"This first novel by Ann Wertz Garvin is fresh, ironic, and psychologically intense. If you're interested in the best in women's fiction—this suspenseful, quirky, humorous story of a well-meaning woman's reverberating effect on her neighbor's life is certainly that and more."

—Jacquelyn Mitchard, *New York Times* bestselling author of *The Deep End of the Ocean*

"What a great book! In turns poignant and funny, *On Maggie's Watch* is a delightful and compelling read with unexpected plot twists and many laugh-out-loud moments."

—Patricia Wood, author of *Lottery*

"*On Maggie's Watch* is equal parts compelling, entertaining, and poignant—a story that tackles a serious topic and leaves readers questioning the way they judge others."

—Holly Kennedy, author of *The Penny Tree* and *The Tin Box*

# On Maggie's Watch

ANN WERTZ GARVIN

BERKLEY BOOKS, NEW YORK

**THE BERKLEY PUBLISHING GROUP**
**Published by the Penguin Group**
**Penguin Group (USA) Inc.**
**375 Hudson Street, New York, New York 10014, USA**
Penguin Group (Canada), 90 Eglinton Avenue East, Suite 700, Toronto, Ontario M4P 2Y3, Canada
(a division of Pearson Penguin Canada Inc.)
Penguin Books Ltd., 80 Strand, London WC2R 0RL, England
Penguin Group Ireland, 25 St. Stephen's Green, Dublin 2, Ireland (a division of Penguin Books Ltd.)
Penguin Group (Australia), 250 Camberwell Road, Camberwell, Victoria 3124, Australia
(a division of Pearson Australia Group Pty. Ltd.)
Penguin Books India Pvt. Ltd., 11 Community Centre, Panchsheel Park, New Delhi—110 017, India
Penguin Group (NZ), 67 Apollo Drive, Rosedale, North Shore, 0632, New Zealand
(a division of Pearson New Zealand Ltd.)
Penguin Books (South Africa) (Pty.) Ltd., 24 Sturdee Avenue, Rosebank, Johannesburg 2196,
South Africa

Penguin Books Ltd., Registered Offices: 80 Strand, London WC2R 0RL, England


Cover design by Lesley Worrell
Cover photo by Ben Fink Photo Inc. / Getty Images
Book design by Laura K. Corless



PRINTING HISTORY
Berkley trade paperback edition / November 2010

Library of Congress Cataloging-in-Publication Data

Garvin, Ann Wertz.
On Maggie's watch / Ann Wertz Garvin.
p. cm.
ISBN 978-0-425-23678-9 (alk. paper)
1. Pregnant women—Fiction. 2. Homecoming—Fiction. 3. Suburban life—Fiction. 4. Neighborhood watch programs—Fiction. 5. Strangers—Fiction. 6. Control (Psychology)—Fiction. 7. Wisconsin—Fiction. I. Title.
PS3607.A78289O52 2010
813'.6—dc22
2010011721

PRINTED IN THE UNITED STATES OF AMERICA

10 9 8 7 6 5 4 3 2 1

For Julie, Meghan, Mom, Dad,
and of course, Ella.

# *Acknowledgments*

Gratitude is not really payment enough for the kind of support an author receives from friends, family, and professionals while writing a novel. There should be a brass band, a granting of wishes, or, at the very least, a promise of clean arteries.

Still, knowing this, I offer my sincerest thank-you to so many people. To the warm and gracious Eve Bridburg, my agent, who functioned as writing professor, friend, and matchmaker; and to the gentle and insightful Jackie Cantor and the rest of the team at Berkley who "get me" and who will forever be known to me as the people who made my dream come true.

As a new writer, I leaned heavily on veterans: Michael Neff, author and founder of the New York Pitch and Shop Conference; Catherine Adams, brilliant book doctor and friend at Inkslinger.com; and the lovely Jacquelyn Mitchard, whose friendship and deep caring has warmed me mightily and often.

And then there are the girlfriends who knew me when: Linda Wick, Tammy Scerpella, and Ingrid Gabriel, who for decades have urged me to write, and when I did, only smiled and offered a knowing and nonjudgmental "I told you so." My early readers, Tonya Talbert, Kara Roism, Laura Carpenter, Cristy Jefson, Carolyn Bach, Teri Osgood, Elyse Tebon, Bev Fergus, and Mona Beckham, supported me through every single blind step I took and never once said, "Oh, would you just shut up." Not once. Bless them.

And when I finally finished the novel, Todd and Katy Labeau and Boone Sesvold at Silicon Prairie put me online, and Len Rubel and Matt Boatright-Simon created a film version of me so much nicer than the actual me. That kind of magic and generosity is unfathomable.

That leads me to the source of my strength and whatever talent I may have. My greatest devotion goes to my parents, Fred and Eleanor Wertz; and to my brothers, Jonathan and Ray, who were my sturdy springboards in life.

Then, and finally, to John P. Garvin. With his intelligence, humor, and love, we created a family. And to our daughters, my twin soul mates, Julie and Meghan. Without these girls I would never have really understood love, or a good milk-through-the-nose joke.

So, to you all, I offer the words of Shakespeare: "I can no other answer make but thanks, And thanks, and ever thanks."

# *Rebel Without a Peanut Allergy*

Wash your hands and say your prayers, 'cause Jesus and germs are everywhere!"

Maggie Finley smiled at her best friend and rolled her eyes. "Tell me you did not just make that up, Julia."

"God, no. I heard it on that country-western music station. One of those Judd girls said it. But it's perfect, don't you think?"

Sitting in a wicker chair with her hand on her seven-months-pregnant shelf of a belly, Maggie said, "You can't use that slogan at a Catholic church. It's blasphemous."

Julia shoved a blond strand of hair off her forehead with the back of her hand and said, "No, it's not. It's the perfect marriage of hygiene and religion. If you're going to be on the food-safety committee, sweetie, you've got to start thinking outside the box." The two women sat on Julia's sunporch, surrounded by markers, poster board, and water bottles. It was the only place in her house not occupied by her sons' wet swimming trunks, plastic action figures, and shoes without laces.

"I didn't ask to be put on the committee. *You* volunteered my services. Besides, the parish doesn't want a full-scale movement against bacteria. They just need someone to make a poster for the pancake breakfast. Something with bullet points. You know, 'Don't bring desserts with peanuts and don't cough on the forks.' "

"You don't know what they want because you didn't come to the first meeting," Julia pointed out.

"From what I understand, the first meeting was bingo night."

"I love bingo night. It's all about comfortable shoes, a good marker, and the potential of winning a canister of caramel corn. We talked about bacteria at the break."

"You're right, that sounds so official. How could I *not* want to be involved?"

"Look, Maggie, the parish needed a fund-raiser. You wanted to get involved. As I remember, you said"—here Julia sat up straight and linked her fingers together in front of her, yin-yang fashion, resembling a Quaker ready to give an oration—" 'I want to use my energies for the betterment of the community.' "

"I did not look like that," Maggie said, smiling and looking irritated at the same time. "I *do* want to get involved, but I was hoping for something a little broader than taking a stand against germs and tree nuts."

"Don't underestimate the tree nut. The tree nut will be the death of us all."

"You're a big bratty kid, Julia."

"A bratty kid with saggy boobs," Julia said, adjusting herself. "No offense, Maggie, but I don't need your help." She pointed to her poster and said, "Look, my peanut has tiny shoes and he's walking toward the exit with the hand sanitizer bottle."

Maggie stood and gazed past the wooden, backyard play structure and plastic yellow slide to the neighboring houses. As if from the same family, the houses all had similar features with only slight differences. A playhouse here, a feeble arborvitae privacy hedge there. All seemed to invite in the American Dream without promising too much individuality or too much success. The American median. As she bit a nonexistent hangnail for the hundredth time, she said, "I need something to keep me busy. To distract me. I can't stop thinking about Ella."

Suddenly uncharacteristically serious, Julia moved

closer to Maggie's side. "You've had a really hard couple of years," she said. "Why don't you try to relax a little? Just take care of yourself."

The shadows under Maggie's eyes seemed to become more noticeable with the mention of the last twenty-four months. "That's what I'm trying to do. Take care of myself while keeping busy."

Julia placed a strong arm around Maggie's shoulder and touched her forehead to her friend's temple. "You don't think an immunology think tank will help you, huh?"

"No, I don't think so. I need something that makes me feel safer. Helps me obsess less about this baby's chances."

"What about Martin?"

Maggie pursed her lips at the mention of her husband's name. "What about him?"

"Is he helping?"

"If working is helping, then yeah, he's helping like a fiend." She laughed mirthlessly. "Every time I bring up Ella, the funeral, or being afraid, he looks like I poked him with a sharp stick."

Julia sighed. "Sometimes I dream about poking my husband with a sharp stick, but I'm afraid the poking would become a stabbing motion, and the next thing you know, I'd be sharing a cell with Lorena Bobbitt."

"Oh, she's not in jail. I saw her on *Oprah* this year."

"God bless her."

"I just want to know that moving home was the best thing for us."

"Your moving back has been the best thing for me." Julia squeezed her friend closer and dropped her arm. "I missed you when you were living in Minneapolis. Are we going to the book signing tonight?"

"Yeah, definitely," Maggie said. "But that's not enough to distract me either."

Julia sighed and said, "Okay, let me think. Maybe you could go work at the food pantry, or help the DNR get rid of the ash borer—that nasty bug eating all our trees—or better yet, volunteer for the Neighborhood Watch."

"There's a Neighborhood Watch?"

"Well, not anymore. You'd have to revamp it," Julia said. "It folded. We used to have great potlucks. We'd spend fifteen minutes talking about dog-poo pickup and then Lou Loomis would grill the brats."

Maggie raised her eyebrows at this new possibility.

Julia returned to her poster and sketched a flipping pancake on a skillet, shared a look with her old friend, and said, "You're always complaining about how everything went to pot when you moved away. Now you're back; here's your chance. Spruce us up."

"We do need some sprucing," Maggie admitted.

"Prevention is the key."

"I'd be perfect for that. The other day I walked past that abandoned gas station on Main. Someone had rearranged the letters on the *free bag of donuts and hot coffee* sign to read *free douche bag here.* So I took a bunch of the letters and threw them in one of those huge green Dumpsters."

"Hey, I saw that. Now it says *free dog here*. I remember wondering what that was about, thinking 'Oh, good, a new pet store.' "

As if to herself, Maggie said, "Prevention is the key. A neighborhood without crime."

"You always *were* afraid of robbers." Julia smiled at the memory. "You couldn't sleep over at my house until your mom came and went through the drill. *No, there are no robbers in this town. No, no robbers in the next town. All the robbers are in New York City at a robber convention, where they learn to take money very quietly, leaving the nice people alone.*"

"Our streets could be the kind of streets they were when we were growing up. Playing kick the can at night, riding bikes during the day. No worries." Maggie sighed a dreamy sigh and pressed her hands lovingly to her stomach. "Safe."

"You wouldn't have to do much. You could resurrect the Watch, elect a president, and let other people do the work." Julia blew the eraser bits away from the penciled-in syrup bottle on the poster and said, "There you have it."

"There you have it," Maggie repeated, as if it was all decided. "No longer will I be a rebel without a cause."

Julia said, "A rebel without a peanut allergy."

The bells chimed prettily as Maggie pushed open the bookstore doors and breathed in the scent of new books and coffee. Her favorites. She spotted Julia, waiting near the entrance, engrossed in a photography book.

"Check this out." Julia slid the glossy coffee-table book in her direction. "Hot firemen."

"That's totally redundant."

"Totally. Look at this one." She pointed to a photograph of a shirtless man, holding a kitten, dressed only in fluorescent green baggie fireproof pants. He had dirt on his face and his helmet was cocked at a jaunty angle.

"You're too easy, Julia."

"You're just saying that because you knew me in high school."

"Everyone knew you in high school."

"Very funny. God, look at those abs."

"Doesn't Steven have abs like that?"

"I haven't seen Big Steven's abdominal muscles since—well, actually, I've never seen Big Steven's abs."

Maggie shut the book and grabbed Julia's elbow. "Come on. Let's go get a seat."

"My painters kind of look like that," Julia said as she let herself be dragged over to the chairs set up at the other end of the store.

"They do? That's good, because they're sure taking their time getting your house done."

"Come see for yourself. They take off their shirts around one."

"Coo, coo, ca-choo, Mrs. Robinson." Maggie laughed. "Now you're kinda creeping me out."

"I'm kind of creeping myself out," Julia admitted. "Steven's out of town so much now we hardly ever park the bus, if you know what I mean. Mostly that's okay, but occasionally I get the urge." She elbowed Maggie and leered.

"You are a juvenile."

"You are a prude."

"Who's watching the boys tonight?" Maggie asked.

"Daphne, our neighbor's daughter. That's why I can't stay too long. She may be able to run the hurdles but she's no match for my boys."

At the book table in the back of the store, Maggie and Julia mingled with the other, mostly female readers, waiting for their favorite author to come out. Maggie picked up a hardcover, lifted it to her nose, breathed in its scent. She looked at the author's photograph and tucked it under her arm. She lifted another book and asked, "Did you ever read this one?"

"That's the one with the kidnapping in it, right? I just couldn't. I heard nothing bad happened to the kid, but I was pregnant with Little Steven at the time and Mikey was just a toddler. I couldn't even bear the thought that kidnappers existed in the world, let alone read a story with one in it."

"It was a good book," Maggie said.

Julia grabbed Maggie's arm playfully. "You know how it is when you're pregnant," she said. "You kind of lose your mind with horror and possibility. I was completely obsessed with washing my hands; a kidnapper was fear beyond the realm. When bacteria are your terrorists, kidnappers are like a nuclear war."

"If you kill all the bacteria, there's always the peanut allergy, though."

"Just another kind of kidnapper."

Taking their seats a few rows back from the front, Maggie said, "I went home today and did some research on Neighborhood Watches."

"What'd ya find out?"

"There's lots of great information online. Like safety tips, things to watch out for, how to create a safety net."

Julia shrugged. "It's not like we're the nexus of crime here in Elmwood, Wisconsin. I mean, what are we really talking about here?"

Maggie floundered a little, trying to think of a recent

crime, something to validate her fears, her need for safety. "I don't know. I'm just getting started."

"It's not like we live in the big city, where there are sex offenders everywhere. Besides, these days, you can check online for those."

"You can find sex offenders online?"

Julia said, "Yeah, but I doubt we have any here. If I were you, my first order of business would be those skateboarders on the post office handicap ramp."

Absently Maggie said, "Skateboarders?"

"Those kids scare the crap out of me. Especially the one with the huge grommet in his ear. I'm afraid he's going to crash into me and break my hip."

"Who are you kidding? If he hit you, Julia, you'd break his arm. When did they put sex offenders online?"

Julia waved her hand. "I don't know. Who cares?"

"I don't think I want to check for offenders."

"Talk about creepy."

Maggie shuddered. "I definitely don't want to know."

"Listen, Mags, you don't have to dredge up crime to have a Watch. Send a few emails. Pretty soon you won't have time to round up all the peanuts in the county and wrap them in latex, you'll have a newborn."

"I can't even think about it."

Julia frowned and pushed a lock of hair behind her ear and said, "Wouldn't it be great if you could give sex offenders a peanut allergy? Then all you'd have to do is put a peanut in your child's pocket. Mothers everywhere could rest easy."

In bed, with the lavender coverlet pulled to her chin, Maggie stared at the ceiling. Martin, oblivious, snored next to her, his hair a mix of frizz and curl. She swallowed hard. A series of remembered movie scenes paraded through her thoughts. Masked men, frightened children, unlocked doors. Maggie pushed herself out of bed and grabbed her robe from the hook behind the door. She rushed through the house checking locks, sliding window clasps into place, pulling shades down. In the kitchen, she touched her hand to her belly, removed the water pitcher from the fridge, and took a long sip directly from the spout. Maggie waited for the rush and tumble of limbs inside. Reassurance.

Glancing around, she silently moved into what doubled as a home office and guest room and stared down at the dark screen of her computer. Tentatively she touched the mouse and the machine came to life.

## *Take a Bite Out of Crime*

TWO WEEKS LATER

Dressed for her morning walk and standing on the front stoop of Julia's house, Maggie licked her lips and pulled her zippered jogging top over her protruding belly. Julia leaned in toward Maggie's face.

"Maggie Finley, are you wearing lipstick?"

Something about the way Julia said this brought Maggie back to her childhood. *Maggie Elizabeth*, her mother used to say, *are you wearing yesterday's underwear?*

"You are such a prissy shit," Julia continued, but she was smiling as she said it. "You want to talk about some emergency, but you pause to touch up your lips? That's what I've always liked about you; you've got your priorities straight." She stood with the sun shining in her eyes, her hands on her hips, and an amused/disgusted expression on her face. "Don't tell me, let me guess. You're wearing Avon's Pinktabulous lipstick with a plan to switch to Mocha Madness later for grocery shopping."

"No, this particular color is called, oddly enough, Prissy Shit," Maggie replied, trying out the obscenity, pressing it to the roof of her mouth. "And just because I like you so much, I bought you your own signature color. It's called Potty Mouth, and it was on special this week."

Smiling like a proud profanity coach, Julia shook her head. "It's nine o'clock on a Monday morning. Who do you think is going to see your makeup? The only people at home are mothers trying to get their hineys in shape to get pregnant again."

"That's where you're wrong, Julia," Maggie said. "There are lots of people home doing all kinds of things you might be interested in. In fact, I'll show you. Let's walk."

Julia started to move in one direction, but Maggie touched her arm and said, "No, this way."

Julia shrugged. "Is this about getting me to join your Neighborhood Watch? Because if it is, sell it somewhere else, sweetie. There's no effing way I'm going to a convention of legally justified busybodies. I just suggested it to keep you busy *thinking* about it, not actually *doing* it."

Maggie glanced at Julia and said, "You might change your mind after today."

"No, I won't. What if I found out that Bill Bauersox wears his wife's underwear? Then I'll have to find Little Steven a new piano teacher. I don't have that kind of time. Besides, I don't want to meet any more of my neighbors. I went to the community potluck Christmas party and that was painful enough, even without the Peeping Tom agenda."

"I know almost as many people as you do. And that's not counting the people from the old days."

"But I like my regular old people. I don't want new people. I just want to be part of the scenery and live my life with all the names I already have phone numbers for. Your moving back here has just about made the landscape perfect for me."

Maggie smiled at the compliment.

"All right already—get on with it," Julia said. "What are you so twitchy about that you couldn't tell me on the phone? What are you holding?"

Maggie held up a bundle of purple papers. "Flyers. You're looking at the new president of the Neighborhood Watch," she said, wagging the notices in front of Julia. "I'm delivering information for the next meeting. I want to set up a calling tree and a schedule."

Julia shook her head. "Of course you do. If I didn't like you so much, I wouldn't be able to stand you. When did this all happen?"

They had been walking at a brisk pace when Maggie

stopped and pulled Julia to the side so they were standing directly in front of each other. "I took it over about a week ago. I found out something about someone in our neighborhood."

Julia tilted her head with exasperation and said, "A few mailboxes are used for batting practice and you want to set up a dragnet."

"This is more than vandalizing mailboxes." Pausing for maximum effect, Maggie cleared her throat and, with a look of stony, sure-to-impress triumph, said, "We have a sexual predator living among us."

Julia gave a kind of incredulous sputter at Maggie's serious expression. "Among us? You should see your face." And then she realized what Maggie had actually said. "Wait. What are you talking about?"

Maggie spoke as quickly and clearly as possible. "I checked out the Department of Corrections' website and there he was: a picture, address, everything."

"What? We have a pervert in our neighborhood? Where? Who is it? What'd he do?"

"See, I knew you'd be interested." Maggie swallowed and went on. "I only just found him. His name is Craig Tyson, and I haven't seen him in person. The federal government has lists online of all the people convicted of some sort of sexual assault. They even post the addresses. And Craig Tyson lives on *this* street. Hemlock Street."

Maggie saw herself then, seated in front of her computer screen. She had scrutinized the young man staring out at her. He was younger than the other offenders on the site. An untidy, full beard covered his face and his curly hair fell just below his jaw. Craig Tyson. Third-degree sexual assault.

Glancing around her, frowning at the closed front doors, the dried lavender wreaths, and the brass doorknockers, Julia rubbed her forehead. "I've heard about the website, but I haven't looked at it. It's just too creepy to think about."

Maggie opened her mouth in surprise. "You knew?"

"I didn't realize they actually posted addresses."

With her eyes theatrically wide, Maggie nodded. "Well, they do! If everyone knows about this site, why aren't people doing something?"

Julia pulled her eyes from a mailbox shaped like a mallard duck and trained her gaze on Maggie's face. "What would you have them do? I've got to be honest with you, you're freaking me out here. Do you know what this guy actually did?"

Maggie remembered that he wore a thoughtful expression in the photo, with a tilt to his head, as if he were considering something vaguely puzzling and maybe even a bit humorous. It was a balanced face, but his eyes, behind black plastic frames, were tipped with . . . what? Sadness? Guilt? What had he done?

"No, but I'm going to keep an eye on him. I can tell you that. Well, me and the Neighborhood Watch, I hope."

"Slow down." She touched Maggie's arm. "Does Martin know about all of this?"

"No! He'd tell me to relax and forget about it." Maggie bit her lip. "You know how Martin is; he thinks marriage is about staying on top of the water, not digging your oar too deep. Besides, he and I have bigger fish to fry." Maggie gestured to her belly. As if presenting Julia with the ultimate gift, Maggie said, "So, you're the first. Besides, I don't want to tell other people until I know what I want to do with him."

"*Do* with him?"

Maggie looked away, fiddled with the drawstring on her pants. "I mean, you know, how to handle telling people."

Julia pushed her sunglasses up onto the perch of her sun visor and took another look at Maggie's set jaw. "Maggie, you are not going to *do* anything with him."

"No, I know, of course not. Besides, you know me. I'm not big on confrontation." Slapping the flyers with the back of her hand, she added, "That's why we have the Neighborhood Watch. As it stands, it's a totally slipshod operation run entirely by a grandmother who does daycare and works at Walmart part-time. You know that one with the mustache who shouts, 'Price check,' as if she doesn't have a microphone?"

"Yeah, I know her. Wait, can I say something?"

Maggie held up her hand. "So, I met with her and asked how often the Neighborhood Watch members meet, and she said, get this, they had one meeting and now they do everything on email. Julia, they don't even have a meeting schedule. There's no patrolling agenda, no mission statement, no five-year plan."

Julia looked sideways at Maggie. "What? No five-year plan?"

"Just listen. I asked if she would consider letting me take over, and she handed me a folder with a partial phone list and a dry-cleaning coupon." Maggie shook her head. "Unreal. So, here's what I'm thinking. I want to set Elmwood's program apart from the national organization. First off, we need something better than the National Crime Prevention's 'Take a Bite Out of Crime.' It's too stuffed-animal-meets-petty-theft. Crime is not something to be trivialized by an artist's rendering of McGruff, the kinder, gentler crime dog. How about this?" Maggie increased her pace and held her hands out expressively. " 'Take No Prisoners' silk-screened in fuchsia on a green camouflage background. Maybe McGruff should be a raven. Quoth the raven, 'Nevermore.' Get it?"

"Okay, wait a minute." Julia paused and repeated Maggie's words. "Are you serious? 'Quoth the raven'? Since when did you become this crime go-getter?"

"Since today. Since I found this guy is living on my street. I'm pregnant. I am not going to bring a child into this world knowing that my neighborhood is not entirely safe. We moved home for a reason."

Maggie said this like she had thought it over. As if she had considered real possibilities, as if she knew what it meant to protect a child, as if she had some kind of plan. In truth, none of this was true. She was freewheeling. High on her newfound confidence. Confidence that was building with each rushed statement. Each fearless fact.

"Listen, this guy lives across the street." Maggie tilted her head to indicate the house diagonally across from where they stood, and then whispered, "C'mon." She started crossing the road, heading for the 1920s bungalow with taupe siding and sage green shutters.

Julia looked both ways and hurried to catch up. "Stop. Where are you going?"

Ignoring Julia's frantic whispered calls, Maggie checked the address—56 Hemlock Street. As she walked up the cement front steps onto a wooden porch, she read *Welcome* on the mat at the base of the door. There was an American flag painted on the mailbox. She curled a flyer into a neat spiral and slid it into the screen-door handle. Taking a breath at the front door, she made a fist to knock, changed her mind, and dropped her hand.

Julia stood on the sidewalk with an expression of bewildered anxiety on her face. She looked at the house and then at Maggie before she spoke with restraint. "Come down from there, honey," she said, as if Maggie were her child, sitting on a rock next to a rattle snake.

Maggie called out to Julia, "Don't you love the color of this paint?" Without warning, she turned, deadheaded a geranium sitting in a large clay pot on the porch and tossed the top into the bushes. She watched it drop and disappear from sight.

"You want to stay and do some gardening, darling?" Julia gave a nervous laugh and grabbed her friend's arm. Maggie turned slightly to cast a glance over her shoulder, and there it was, a gentle movement of a gauzy curtain, the shadow of a human form. With a fierceness that was new to her, she spit back a whispered warning toward the window: "I know you're here."

Listen, Maggie, I don't like you as suburban avenger. You leave this guy alone, stay off his front porch, and no more flyer deliveries, either." Julia had Maggie by the elbow and was trying hard not to swat her behind like she might with her five-year-old son. "You don't know anything about him or his situation. What if he's dangerous? Wait, he *is* dangerous, we already know that. God, I can't believe we are talking about this."

Maggie looked back over her shoulder. "Do you think he saw us? I thought I saw the curtains move." Her cheeks were pink and she was slightly breathless.

Julia followed Maggie's eyes back down the street. "You have lost your mind." She pulled Maggie across the street and around the corner before stopping and facing her. "The Maggie I grew up with was afraid of pissing off a waiter by ordering off the menu. Who are you?"

Maggie squared her shoulders and said, "I know this is not the *me* you're used to. Maggie the peacekeeper. Maggie the insecure. But I'm tired of sitting back and letting everyone else determine my life for me."

"Tell me again how this sex-offender guy, this Greg-whatever-his-name-is is trying to determine your life. I am assuming that until today he didn't know you were alive."

"His name is Craig—Craig Tyson—and he may not be *determining* my life today, but he lives in my town, in my neighborhood, and I can't have this information and not do something about it."

"Why do you keep saying that?"

"Right after we talked, I saw this YouTube talk show devoted entirely to sex offenders. There was a police specialist. It was like he was speaking directly to me. He said, 'Become an investigator. Be more paranoid, not less. Be proactive.' I figured if the cops were worried, I better wake up and smell the predators."

Julia's lips thinned into an irritated grimace, and she said, "I think it's safe to say that you have never been deficient in paranoia."

"I can't tell you how disturbing that website is. It's like the Sears, Roebuck Christmas Catalog of Parental Fears, each electronic page with a photograph and a price. I kept wondering if I had seen any of them skulking at the grocery store, in the toothpaste aisle. Or circling around the elementary school parks, or peering out of shabby apartment windows. I feel like I have to do something."

"Look, I get it," Julia said. "I hate that these people exist, but you, personally, can't get rid of them."

Maggie put her chin up. "Why. Why not me?"

"Well, it's illegal, for one thing. You're too pregnant to be Wyatt Earp, for another."

"I've got two months. That's enough time to get started. Besides, I feel great." Swallowing, she added, "I'm never going to do nothing again."

Julia paused and looked at her friend's face. Maggie looked tired and stressed. Softening, Julia said, "I know you know this, but it bears repeating. Ella didn't die because you were somehow too passive."

"I just think," Maggie said quietly, "that if I'd paid more attention, researched warning signs, been more aware of the dangers . . ." Maggie's voice trailed off. Starting again, she said quietly, "I worry that this baby may be swimming in a poisonous sea. A beautiful pea trapped in a spoiled pod."

"There is nothing wrong with your pod. No one is more worthy of a child than you."

"I need some girl power, and taking charge makes me feel like I can do this pregnancy better. That I *am* worthy this time."

"I don't know, Mags. Maybe the Neighborhood Watch presidency is"—Julia paused, selecting her words like they were perfect chocolate truffles—"too much for you right now."

"Too much? It's the least I can do." Maggie pushed a strand of hair out of her face and let out a puff of a laugh. "But if it makes you feel better, I have no intention of doing anything crazy, I promise. Do you think I would jeopardize this pregnancy by doing something truly risky? I didn't quit my job, move home, try yoga just to . . ." She faltered.

"Honey, I'm just saying, the old Maggie never liked the stress of center stage."

"You're right. I don't like being in charge. I excel at the planning and organization part. I like to think of myself as the file cabinet rather than the mouthpiece of meetings. That's why I need you to co-chair. You're the people person."

Julia had a tired expression on her face. "I'm not putting any energy into criminals. I don't want to be the head private eye of this ZIP code. I'd maybe have come to the first meeting just to see the freak show. Now . . . well, I don't know."

"You'd come if you looked at the website. Plus, this is a chance to make sure nothing happens to our children." Maggie attempted to lighten the moment. "Besides, you're as protective of your kids as I am. I see you with your boys. Did you forget I know about safety camp?"

"That is a low blow. It was Big Steven's idea for the boys to go to safety camp. I thought it would be a little stop, drop, and roll followed by a juice box. I didn't know they were going to cover everything from condoms to farm safety, or I would have put a stop to it."

"Oh, c'mon, it wasn't that bad."

"No?" Julia lifted one eyebrow and looked at her friend. "Michael was fine. He's eight, he can process stuff. But Little Stevie was a wreck after the whole experience. It was the farm friends puppet show with the stuffed horse catching his hoof in the combine that put him over the edge. Now, every time a car starts, he flinches. It's been a month and he's only just now starting to leave the toaster plugged in at night. Christ, he sounds just like you lately: *You can never be too safe, Mama!* It's totally weird."

Their walk had taken them full circle. Maggie looked up and noticed that a bird had made a nest up under one of the eaves of Julia's house. "Okay, you've made your point. I promise to keep it cool. But I won't promise to give up the Neighborhood Watch."

"One of the great things about you has always been your sweet-natured dependability. If you're going to start wearing a superhero costume, I might just have to crush pills into your coffee in the morning."

Maggie laughed and waved her off. "Get in line. Martin has dibs on my coffee."

## *Geraniums, Gazebos, and American Flags*

Seated in her home office, Maggie lifted the hair off the back of her neck and settled in front of her computer. Unable to resist, she went right back to the Wisconsin sex offender website: first- and second-degree sexual assault, no child involved, child involved. After a moment, she shuddered and then began silently counting, as she had the day before, and the day before that, twenty-three local sex offenders living in her hometown. Twenty-three names with ten aliases. Her arms dropped and she cradled her belly.

"What are you doing in the office?"

"Oh, God!" Maggie shouted, rolling back and bouncing the exercise ball she sat on. She quickly minimized the open webpage and stood, blocking Martin's view of the computer.

"You scared me, Martin!" she said, as she moved around the edge of the oak desk. "What are you doing home?"

"I didn't mean to startle you. I forgot my phone." He held up his cell phone for her to see.

Maggie bent to tie her jogging shoes and looked through her bangs at him with a half smile. "So you're spying on me? Keeping tabs now that I'm a stay-at-home full-time gestator?"

"Is that a word? *Gestator?* One who gestates?" He reached for her shoulders.

She stood and adjusted the waistband of her shorts. "Seriously, sweetie, I can't relax when you're constantly making sure I'm relaxing."

"I was checking *in*—not checking *up*—on you. I wanted a kiss good-bye from my wife. The wife I thought I'd find with her feet up, eating a scone."

Smiling, she said, "That's me all right. I'm all about pastries and pedicures while waiting for the next Junior League meeting." Dropping the corners of her mouth, she said, "I know there are people who can quit working and be happy. But I'm not one of them."

"Right now, this pregnancy is your work. Maybe you should just *try* relaxing in your robe or going for lunch with your mom or Julia," he said with his I-know-how-to-fix-this look. "Isn't that why you quit work and we moved back here?"

"We did *not* move here so I could learn how to lounge in my pajamas." Maggie sighed as if having to review, once again, a particularly difficult math equation that required a simple solution. "You know why we're here." With a slight shake of her head, she continued, "Why we left every stained memory of our life up there. Bus exhaust, cigarettes, and rain on Hennepin Avenue. Those hospital doors. Ugh."

Martin released a long, slow breath and blinked a touch too long, "Okay, don't unwind. Drink your decaf. You win."

Martin stepped around toward the computer, and Maggie, using her belly like she was setting a pick on the basketball court, stepped squarely in front of her husband. She placed both hands on his chest and let the middle finger of her right hand rest softly in the hollow of his throat. His arms carefully moved around her. "I don't want to win," she said, breathing in his signature scent of Ivory soap and Old Spice. "I'm sorry I'm so edgy. You know how I get." She cleared her throat and fiddled with the button on his shirt. "It's Ella. I need to figure out how to keep this next one safe. Unharmed, in and out."

Martin's tension showed in his temple. He didn't want

to talk about it. The year and a half of psychologists, support groups, and grief counselors had taken its toll. All of the experts they'd met after Ella's death seemed to hover overhead with notepads opened, pencils poised. Martin paused, looked into his wife's face, and tugged gently on her shoulder-length brown hair. Moving her oversize T-shirt out of the way and resting his hands on the bare skin of her belly, he said, "I want to keep this one safe, too. I just need to remember Ella quietly and move forward."

She took his chin in her hand and gently pulled his face to hers. "Not everyone is content to just . . ." She pinched the words to a close. Clearing her throat, she started again. "I'm sorry; I'm just jittery. Remember what the doctor said—that I need to take care of myself in my own way."

Stepping back, he put his foot on the blue exercise ball and bounced it with his heel. "You know we can afford a desk chair. You said yourself this core-strength business is probably all pomp and very little circumstance where the delivery is concerned."

Maggie watched as his attention faded, and she exhaled with a knowing smile on her face. "You'll be happy for every muscle fiber when the time comes again." A shared memory materialized between them—a hospital bed, a pair of silver forceps, blue surgical scrubs. Finding no comfort there, Maggie shoved the fatigue of the fight aside and looked at her watch. Suddenly impatient for him to leave, she said, not unkindly, "You'd better go if you're going to make your meeting. I'll be fine. Go fix some computers." Like a child released from detention, he gave her hand a sheepish squeeze and left.

Maggie stepped around her desk and looked out the window into the hushed street. Martin was already checking his cell phone as he ducked his head and got into the car. Her gaze followed him as he backed down the driveway and out into the streets of their charming ZIP code. Their charming town. Elmwood, Wisconsin. Population 12,344. Geraniums, gazebos, and American flags.

Back at her desk, she frowned at her computer and gave the oversize rubber ball a kick. It retaliated by banging back into her lower legs. She sat and reached for her coffee. Empty. Her one allotted cup a day, gone. Pushing her mug out of the way, she grabbed her mouse and clicked, and the screen came to life.

One by one Maggie opened the file of each local sex offender listed online. She studied the hairlines and eyeglasses frames, trying to place them. She chewed the ragged cuticle on her thumbnail and jiggled her foot. Straightening the notepad and pencils on her desk, she read the flyer again: *Come to the Neighborhood Watch meeting. Refreshments will be served. Make YOUR neighborhood safe!!* Maggie raked her fingers over the edges like a dealer at a casino and placed her palm down in the center of the stack.

The telephone rang, and she yanked her hand away as if the flyers were hot. She hesitated for a moment, picked up the receiver, and pressed Talk.

"Martin?"

The voice on the other end had a very nasal, very un-Martin-like quality to it.

"Hello, this is Beverly Finker calling for Maggie McGuire Finley? I opened the door this morning? To get the paper?" Though her statements came out as questions, Beverly Finker didn't pause for answers. "I found your Neighborhood Watch flyer in the handle of my door."

Finally, a statement. Maggie waited a beat or two before responding, just to be sure. "Yes, I dropped off several notices this morning. I hope that was all right."

"Oh my, yes. In fact, I'm calling to see how I can help? I would have started something like this years ago? But, my husband, Denny, doesn't like to put our names on petitions and the like? He's afraid of becoming a target? After I read the flyer, I had to call, dangerous or not. 'Beverly,' he always says, 'you've got to think before you proceed.' This time I said, 'Denny? Target or not, it's time for some action.'" There was no question mark on the end of that phrase; Beverly meant business.

"How can I help you, Mrs. Finker?"

"No, sweetie, how can I help you? I've got lots of thoughts. I've kept notes on neighbors for years. Finally, I can put some of my hard work to good use."

"Notes?"

"Yes, notes. There is a lot of suspicious activity in our little township and I've got some ideas. Like, for example, you know that darling of a fountain on the corner of Page and Franklin? Just about once a week some little vandal puts dish soap into it? By morning the whole thing is a frothy mess and the little angel on top 'bout looks rabid. I think this is a perfect situation for a nanny cam, don't you? I'd like to catch the little A-hole who's doing it, I really would."

This sudden foray into profanity, coming from a woman whom she pictured looking like Miss Piggy, threw Maggie. "Oh, well, I . . ." she stuttered. "Well, maybe we can talk about all this at the first meeting."

"That's why I'm calling? I can't make that meeting. Denny has a Knights of Columbus fish fry and I'm in charge of the batter? I was really thinking that we could meet ahead of time and talk about how we could co-run the Neighborhood Watch?"

"Co-run?"

"Yes. Surely you'll be needing some help, considering your pregnancy and all."

Maggie paused. "My pregnancy? How did you know?" And her voice trailed off in surprise.

"I was watching you from the window. I live in the brick house on Wilmington Way. I saw you place the flyer and take off with your friend? I know her. Doesn't she live on Van Buren?"

Unnerved to be the unknown subject of another's scrutiny, Maggie said, "Beverly, can I call you back? I'm right in the middle of something that I really need to get back to."

"Certainly, anytime. I'm retired, so you can call whenever you need to. In the meantime, I'll keep my eyes peeled."

## *Snakes in the Manicured Grasses of Middle America*

Julia stomped up the wooden planks of the front-porch stairs, the sound of her footsteps reverberating in the air. She yanked open the front door, stepped inside the darkened entry, and kickboxed the door shut. Grasping the dead bolt, she slid it into place, paused, and swiftly unlocked the door.

On the way down the hall, she picked up a toy snare drum with a hole in the head and the arm of a robot. She pitched the toys into the first open room, where they clattered to the floor. The robot's hand snapped loose and rolled into a shoe turned on its side. Marching into the family office, Julia took a breath and touched the computer mouse. The screen brightened and her two sons appeared, with their jack-o'-lantern smiles and freckles on their noses. Blondies. Michael had his arm draped around Little Steven's neck, holding him like he was an invertebrate. Both had potbellies, swim goggles on their heads, and sand shovels clutched in their hands. A brief smile skittered across Julia's face.

As she moved her chair closer to the computer, she searched for the Wisconsin Department of Corrections. Dusting the screen with her sleeve as she navigated the website, she scowled at the photos and muttered, "Snakes in the manicured grasses of Middle America."

She checked her watch; Little Steven would be back soon. Moving her pointer straight to Craig Tyson's name, she clicked and waited. His unlined, young face came into view while she secured a piece of blond hair behind her ear and read, "Five-foot-eleven, third-degree sexual assault, life registration."

"Damn right," she whispered.

A loud blast from a car horn broke her concentration. Closing the website, she hurried down the hall. Little Steven struggled with an overlarge backpack to get out of the carpool van as Julia made her way down the sidewalk. Her son held what looked like a giant gob of gum under his arm.

"Hey, Mom. Look, it's my head. We made it in day camp."

Julia took the papier-mâché sculpture from Little Steven as he clambered out of the car and said, "Sure enough, there are your blue eyes, just where they belong, right next to each nostril."

"Yeah, but I only finished one ear and didn't have time to paint my teeth. No biggie, I'm gonna lose 'em all soon anyways."

"Anyway," Julia corrected him. "Run inside and get a snack. I want to talk to Tonya for a second." Julia slid the van door shut and stuck her head inside the passenger-side window.

"Thanks so much for driving, I'll get them tomorrow. Hey, do you have a second? I want to ask you something."

Tonya Talbert pushed her tiny wire glasses up the bridge of her nose and said, "Sure, but only just a second. I have to drop off Sabrina soon or her mother will start calling my cell for updates." She rolled her eyes and nodded to the back of the van where a little girl of about eight sat primly, holding an artful duplication of her little blond, ponytailed head.

"Have you ever gone online to check out the sex offenders who live in this town?"

"God, yeah. There's a bunch of 'em around here."

"I noticed. It's disturbing. I felt like I was checking out a perverse online dating service. Height, weight, and sexual preference included."

Tonya closed her eyes briefly and shook her head.

"I don't get it," Julia said. "How can those people know when garbage day is and not know to keep their hands off children?"

"We don't have any on our street, luckily. I think Tim would personally torch the place if we did."

"Really?" Julia searched Tonya's face for sincerity.

"Well, no, not really, but I do think he would make us move."

Julia gazed over the top of the van. The hydrangeas were blooming, and Mrs. Baggett was digging up her boulevard to plant primroses.

"Maggie Finley is starting a Neighborhood Watch."

"Maggie Finley? Really? That surprises me." Tonya brushed her hair back and checked the rearview mirror. "Let me know if she gets it up and running. I might be interested. I better go. I'll see you tomorrow."

Julia walked back inside and found Little Steven teasing Mr. Tubby, the family cat, with his sock and finishing a breakfast waffle, cold from hours on the counter.

"Hey, buddy, how was day camp?"

"Good," Little Steven answered. "Where's Mikey?"

"Still swimming. We'll go get him in an hour." Julia gazed down on her son's yellow spiraled cowlick, his archless foot, the birthmark on his chin.

With unpracticed nonchalance, Julia embarked on a

conversation she considered as distasteful as liquid cold medicine. "Hey, bud? You know not to talk to people who aren't friends of ours, right?"

Without looking up, he replied, "Yep. Stranger danger. We talked about it in safety camp."

"Good." A breath of relief filtered out her nose. She reached out and brushed his hair away from his forehead; he dodged her and swallowed a wad of cold waffle.

Taking another bite, he asked, "What about the guy who bags our groceries? He says 'hello' all the time. Can I talk to him?" Little Steven's face held an expression of pure innocence—blue eyes, cloudless sky, and guileless little boy.

"Only if me or Daddy's with you. Don't talk to him if you see him on the street."

"That wouldn't be very nice." He looked at Mr. Tubby and giggled, and Julia cracked her knuckles.

"Um, it's important to be kind to people, you're right. I mean, I don't want you to be rude." She looked at the ceiling, searching for parenting instructions, then settled her eyes on her son. "Still, sometimes we don't know very much about people. They might not be as nice as they seem."

"He gave me a balloon. I'm pretty sure the bag guy is nice."

Abruptly Julia stood and said, "No! We don't know that." Mr. Tubby started and scrambled away.

"Geez, Mom, you scared Tubs."

"I'm sorry. It's just that I don't want you talking to people we don't know really, really well."

"You don't have to yell at me." Julia watched as Little Steven walked after the cat, one sock on his foot, one in his hand.

"Freaking Maggie," she hissed. Putting her hand to her head, she strode to the door and flipped the dead bolt into place.

## *A Fearful Drink of a Woman*

"Hey, Mom, can you buzz me in?" Maggie stood outside the tobacco warehouse where her mother lived, now newly converted into stylish condominiums. Across the street stood a grade school with soccer fields and a playground filled with orange tubes, slides, and chin-up bars. The school her child would go to. The condo her child would visit after school for cookies with Grandma.

A squawk of static pushed a metallic voice through the fist-sized speaker at Maggie's chin. "Is that Maggie Finley? My beautiful and successful but rarely seen daughter, Maggie Finley?" The buzzer screeched and the security hinge clicked.

Maggie set her jaw and pulled the dark walnut outer door open. She blinked, allowing her eyes to adjust, and saw a head of brown curls appear around the corner of a sage green hallway. "You make the same lame joke every time I see you," Maggie called, walking toward her mother.

"I'm a very lame, funny woman," she said, reaching out to hug her daughter and pull her inside. "What are you doing in this neck of the woods?"

"I don't think you can use that phrase in a town of twelve thousand, Mom. You make it sound like I had to travel miles to get here."

"Do I need to mention that if I saw you more, it wouldn't feel like you live on the other side of the earth?"

"I just saw you! Besides, you're the one traveling all over the place lately. I told Martin the baby's going to call out 'Grandma' to any brown blur that races by."

Maggie and her mother settled onto a love seat in front of a picture window that framed an ancient crabapple tree. Kicking off her worn Birkenstock sandals, her mother tucked her legs underneath her and pulled her hair up into an impromptu bun with a pencil.

"So, what's up?"

Maggie pulled her leather portfolio forward and displayed a purple flyer from her morning delivery. "Since

I'm reorganizing the Neighborhood Watch, I thought you might come to the first meeting, maybe help me prepare, make some food."

Spinning a large silver and amber ring on the second finger of her left hand, her mother examined the flyer, her eyes filtering down the page.

"When did you start wearing a ring on that hand?" Maggie asked.

"I don't know, not too long ago, I guess."

"You've always kept it bare, I mean, since Dad died."

Her mother glanced without merit at her hand and refocused her attention on Maggie's face. "I thought you were going to organize this online," she said. "What are you planning on doing at this meeting?"

"Discuss neighborhood issues, maybe bring in the police chief for an information session, talk about a schedule for observation." Her mother's dubious expression encouraged Maggie to go into convince mode. "They have these groups all around the country. I think it's time for Elmwood to get on board." She sat up straight, as if she were on a job interview. She reached up to smooth her bangs, stopped, and bit a nail.

"This is what you want to do in the eighth month of your pregnancy? Hand out notices and talk about potential . . . what? Covenant infractions?"

"I sure won't have time after the baby comes, and I'd

like to have some kind of crime-watch network in place before then."

"Is Julia part of this crime club?"

"Probably not. She says it's not her thing."

"I wonder why it's your thing." Her mother sighed and said, "Mix one part disappearing father with two parts barely-hanging-in-there mother, and you get one fearful drink of a woman named Maggie McGuire Finley."

Maggie snapped her head up. "This isn't about you, you know. Not everything is about you."

"No, I know it isn't. But for a really long time, it was nothing but me. Me and your father, that is. Our problems."

"Newsflash: This time it's not." Snatching the flyer from her mother's hand, she said, "Never mind, forget it. I don't know what I was thinking." She started to push the paper back into her portfolio, but then stopped and said, "Oh, what the hell. I'm sorry, Mom."

Her mother touched Maggie's forearm.

"It's just that Julia gave me grief about this already this morning. I expect to get it from Martin when I tell him—he wants a pet wife—and Julia has all the answers. But I didn't expect it from you. I thought maybe you, of all people, might understand my need for safety and for something my husband doesn't have his hands in."

"Don't be so hard on Martin. You two have had a

tough time of it. He just wants to protect you. Besides it's not the idea of the Neighborhood Watch I'm opposed to. I'm just not sure this is the time for it in your life."

"Should I wait like you waited, Mom? Should I just sit on my hands and *make do*? Do nothing?" Her mother's face froze and Maggie lifted her chin. "I've seen that expression before, but you usually reserved it for Daddy." As if sensing a need for cooler temperatures, the air conditioner came on with a light wave of chilly air.

"How long are you going to be mad at me?"

Maggie smiled in spite of herself and dragged her eyes up to her mother's face. "I'm not just angry at *you*, Mom," she said, rotating her head and stretching her neck.

"That's a relief. I'm glad you're spreading it around a little."

Maggie dropped her eyes and laughed. "You should get a dog, Mom. You can forever tell them what to do, and they'll sit on your lap at the end of the day and ask for more."

"Mavis has a dog. One of those damn Labradoodles. Every time I go there, he sticks his nose in my crotch. If I want that kind of reaction when I enter a room, I'll get married again."

Maggie shook her head and rubbed her eyes. "I've gotta go. I'm tired and I love you and I don't want to fight."

Lifting her grin in a way that looked part bittersweet,

part signature charm, her mother said, "That's good, because I hear getting mad at your mother in your eighth month causes spina-snarl-at-ya—the tendency for the baby to duplicate said anger at unpredictable times. I should know."

Maggie stood and fingered her car keys.

Her mother continued, "In case you're interested, Mavis and I are starting a book club, but instead of reading Austen or Tolstoy, we're going to read *People* magazine. It will be all *People* all the time."

Maggie rolled her eyes dramatically.

"What?" Her mother smiled. "Too good for *People*, are you? I bet I get a bigger crowd at my club than you do at yours."

As a child, Maggie's whole world was the loop of road called Covington Place, a left turn going west off Franklin Avenue past Zabrinski's pond. These days Maggie only visited her old haunts when the automated guiding device in her head directed her back to her neighborhood. A homing device as dependable as the one that helped Maggie find her tired insecurities.

Today she drove through town for a reason. She pulled up across from her childhood home. A tiny box of a house seated in the middle of a forgettable lot. Years ago, when her father was around, the possibility of a blustery entrance or angry exit was ever present. A gargoyle perched on a doorframe, ready to pounce. When her father was home, her mother would try to clean up all her jagged personality pieces and roll them into a pie-dough circle. She'd put away her cigarettes, stay off the phone, and cook large meals complete with relish tray and dessert.

With all the forced sunny activity surrounding her father's entrances and exits, Maggie never understood her mother's tears late into the night. At bedtime, Maggie remembered questioning her mother about her sadness, thinking she possibly missed her own mommy.

Maggie wanted assurances that she would never have to leave.

"I don't want to go to college. I want to stay here and live with you," she'd say, smeary-eyed and hopelessly sad for her future, so certain to be lacking in nighttime backrubs and whispered *sleep tights*.

Her mother would rub her back with just the right nail pressure, covering all her itchy spots, and say, "Hush, Mags. You aren't going anywhere tonight. You're just overtired." After turning her wet pillow over to the cool dry side and smoothing her hair away from her face, her mother would take off her sweater and let Maggie sleep with it, inhaling safety, contentment, and citrusy goodness.

These days she knew there was more to safety than

a backrub and a good night's sleep. Pushing against the steering wheel, Maggie sat up in her seat. She hit the electronic door lock and put the car in drive. It didn't take long to reach Tyson's place. There was a large privacy hedge conveniently located in front of the house next door. Maggie pulled over and positioned the van to allow her a clear view of the front porch and driveway. She reached into her bag, secured her hair away from her face with a rubber band, and planted a baseball cap on top of her head. Maggie pulled out a purple flyer from her portfolio, consulted her watch, and recorded the time.

Julia would kill her if she knew what she was doing. She could almost hear her say, "Maggie, they have restraining orders for exactly this kind of thing, you know."

Martin would jump right on that wagon and say, "You are watching too much TV if you think it is okay to hang out in the van, casing free citizens."

Her only goal was to catch a glimpse of Craig Tyson. Maggie repositioned her legs and watched the keys in the ignition shake. For fifteen minutes, Maggie cataloged the activity on the street. One cyclist (over forty), one dog trotting alone, and two mothers strolling by with babies—but no single, bearded men went in or out of the attractive, shuttered bungalow.

She looked at the pen in her hand, clicked it open and closed several times. She grabbed the purple flyer and, on the back, began a list of ideas to get Tyson's attention. *Garbage in front lawn, deflate car tires, remove all solar garden lights, drop bleach on front lawn, steal lightbulb from driveway lamp, send magazine subscriptions, order pizzas for delivery, and paint large yellow P (for predator) at end of driveway.* She considered the list and added *stop Sunday newspaper delivery.*

Maggie jerked her head up and watched as a green sedan peppered with dings pulled into Tyson's driveway. A woman stepped out of the car, slipped her purse onto her shoulder, and reached into the passenger side for a gallon of milk and a thin plastic grocery bag. Moving to a side door by the garage, she pulled the screen door open and knocked with her foot. The woman wore running shoes, blue trousers with an elastic waistband, and a neatly tucked-in yellow blouse. With her hair closely cropped, she looked older than Maggie but not as old as Maggie's mother. She was trim with a smidge of middle-age belly. Sexual Offender Meals on Wheels came to mind and a spark of outrage ignited Maggie as she narrowed her eyes.

Suddenly, the door opened from the inside and Maggie caught a glimpse of a hand and forearm reaching out to take the gallon of milk. Maggie released her breath slowly and waited. The woman walked through the door, then turned and looked toward Maggie. Maggie froze, pulled in her breath and held it until the woman stepped into the house, shutting the door behind her. Maggie sat alert and ready to move for another five minutes before recording: *3:35 p.m.: Man inside. Lives with woman? Who? Does she know?*

Then she picked up her cell phone and called for two family-size pizzas to be delivered to the house in front of her. Pepperoni, sausage, and extra cheese for the sex offender. If she couldn't roust him from the neighborhood, the saturated fat would get him in the long run. *Meals on Wheels, my ass,* she thought. Bon appétit.

# *The Balance Beam*

Maggie fidgeted in her kitchen as she considered the agenda for the first Neighborhood Watch meeting. The light from the window fell on the remnants of her lunch, and she pressed the crumbs of her tuna sandwich into her fingers. Maggie squinted at the sunlight and walked to the sink, rinsed her plate, and reached for her green steno notebook. *Neighborhood Watch* was written at the top of one page. She checked the items on her list: *(1) Roster with emails, (2) Name Game, (3) Calling Tree, (4) Schedule of Observation Dates, (5) Gift Bags? (6) Stop Sign Cookies? (7) Pledge—amend 1970s Girl Scouts' "On my honor, I will try to serve God and my* neighborhood." She scratched off *Pledge* and wrote, *Do not talk about sex of-*

*fender yet. Information pending.* She closed her notebook as Martin walked into the room.

Maggie grabbed a knife, a cutting board on the counter, and a fat avocado in the sink. Chopping a large chunk of white cheese into small squares, she glanced over her shoulder at her husband.

"I hope the Neighborhood Watch meeting goes well tonight. I figure the majority of the responsible neighbors will come." She dropped a handful of cheese into a large metal bowl. The pieces thudded and bounced, hitting the sides. She gambled another quick look at her silent husband. "I thought fondue would be a nice change. No Super Bowl frivolity for these crime watchers. Forget the sausage and cheese plates and big bags o' chips." She smiled at Martin, who was absorbed with pouring milk into a large bowl of sugary cereal.

He picked up a spoon and dunked the bobbing yellow cereal, splashing drips of milk everywhere, then reached for his coffee mug and skated it around the table. Without looking up he said, "Do you really think all this food is necessary?"

"Maybe not, but it gives me something to do with my mind before the meeting and with my hands during the social part of tonight."

Martin pursed his lip and air escaped in a slow steady stream. "I don't get this. How did you get to be in charge of this Neighborhood Watch thing, anyway?"

Standing on her toes, Maggie reached to the back of the cupboard, poking through the jars of spices with red and green tops. "I volunteered a week or so ago. I saw a poster at the library. I called the woman in charge, asked her if she needed some help. It was pathetic, Martin. They *need* my help."

"A treasurer is help. A secretary is help. You're the president. You didn't feel the need to run this by me before making flyers and dropping them all over town?"

She picked up the metal bowl and sat it smartly on the stove top. The clang punctuated her thoughts. "I didn't think I needed to ask permission. Just because we're married doesn't mean I don't get to have a life."

"It's not unfair of me to want to be in the loop. I stopped at Larry's to drop off the weed eater, and he asked me if he was supposed to bring a dish to pass. I didn't know what the hell he was talking about."

"What'd you tell him? The last thing I want is Jell-O salad or some lame seven-layer muck to spoil the food message."

Raising his voice slightly, he said, "What do you think I told him? I told him you would call because, Maggie—and try to pay attention here—I didn't even know we were having a party, let alone a whole George Orwell, Big Sister's watching convention."

Maggie put the knife down and, with exaggerated purpose, slid the cutting board toward the middle of the counter. She pulled out one of the matching kitchen chairs and sat opposite her husband.

She sighed a controlled breath of consolation and said, "I meant to tell you. You've been working so much."

Martin set his jaw and said, "Your not telling me about the Neighborhood Watch is not my fault, Maggie."

"No? Well, I guess I didn't tell you because I was afraid of this exact reaction. I knew you wouldn't want me getting involved. I knew you'd get mad."

Martin looked into the face of his wife and tried again. "If you're looking for something to do before the baby comes, why don't you get started on the nursery? Set up the crib, hire a painter."

"This is not something to do just to pass the time. Besides, I thought we could do those things together." Maggie unconsciously touched her belly, rubbing it in a small circular pattern. Martin pushed his cereal bowl toward the center of the table and the spoon fell out like a top-heavy sailor from a dinghy.

"There's something else I haven't told you."

Martin snapped his head to attention. Maggie quickly added, "Don't worry, this isn't about me. Not really."

"What? What is it?"

"There's a sex offender living on our street."

"Fuck." Martin closed his eyes, rested his elbows on the table, and pushed his palms into his eyes.

Maggie gently touched his leg. "I know it's horrible. Now do you see?"

Martin opened his eyes and stared directly at Maggie. "This might come as a surprise to you, but I'm a computer person. We're all about safety and protection."

Maggie sat back and examined her husband's face. "You know about him?" His expression remained tight, unyielding. "You knew we had a sexual predator living near us and you didn't tell me?"

"I knew about the sex offender database and that there are offenders in our town. I never looked long enough for addresses. I guess I didn't want to know *exactly* where they live."

Maggie backed her chair away from Martin and stood up.

"What were you thinking? You should have told me."

"What good does it do to know where they live?"

"It helps me protect our child, that's what good it does. It tells me where to walk, who to talk to, what routes to avoid."

Dropping his hands to his sides, he said, "You're right. I should have told you. Of course. I'm sorry." He walked to the sink. Maggie imagined he was telling himself not to argue with a very pregnant woman. He was giving her the point, but he didn't mean it.

"What if nobody comes tonight?" he asked. "In my

experience, people like to remain in peaceful ignorance. Maybe no one is all that interested in a Neighborhood Watch."

"There are Neighborhood Watch groups all over the nation in towns quieter than Elmwood. It's not the actual crime that gets people to the meetings. It's the *possibility* of danger. People watch too much TV. You'll see." Maggie smoothed her hair.

"I'm just not sure what organizing a crime networking group is actually going to do for you. If it makes you feel safer, then I suppose I can handle it. The real question is, are you sure you can?" He tried to take Maggie into his arms.

Maggie twisted her lips and dodged his arms. "You think I haven't thought this through? That this is some kind of a whim of mine?"

"Believe me, I *know* you think things through." He rubbed his face with his hands and said, "I just worry."

Maggie shrugged. "I'll make you a deal. If nobody comes, I'll drop the whole thing."

"You'll give up the whole club? No newsletters, no group emails, no informational flyers? Really?"

Maggie nodded, removed her frown, and replaced it with a tiny dimpled grin. "Remember on our wedding day? Your mother said you could have found an easier woman."

"Do you remember what I said to her?"

"'No shit, Sherlock.'"

"That's right. I knew what I was getting into. I just didn't know it would be *every day*. I should have taken classes, studied up."

"I'm not that difficult, if you pay attention."

He stepped forward and kissed Maggie on the lips, and then looked down at her tidy brown hair and matching dark eyes. "You're not exactly easy to read or consistent."

"Nobody is, Martin. People . . . relationships are more complex than that."

"Look, we'll talk more when I get home." He stooped to collect his laptop and a pair of sunglasses.

"You're leaving again? It's Saturday."

"I've got to get to work and solve other peoples' software issues. Ours are on our hard drive and that's going to take some time." Grasping his keys, he turned toward the door.

Maggie took a step toward her husband, stopped, and turned back to the metal bowl on the counter. Quietly, she said, "We could get started today. If you stayed."

Without looking in her direction, he said, "It looks like you've got it covered, as always. I'll see you tonight."

Turning she called to his retreating figure, "Think of tonight as killing two birds with one stone. We get to try new appetizer recipes while creating a safer neighborhood for our children."

Already out the door by this time, the slam of the screen cut off her words. Maggie returned to the sink and gazed into the backyard and thought, *Why is everything in a marriage a negotiation? My father never negotiated anything; he always did just what he wanted. He got drunk, left for weeks on end to who knows where, and then died.*

She remembered watching her mother from a secret space under the stairs with the smell of cleaning supplies and musty paper bags surrounding her. Maggie liked to sit with her bird binoculars, peeking through the cracks in the individual steps, hidden from view in the cramped closet—a dependable, unchanging area in a nervous milkshake world.

Her mother would rhythmically nod at some wisdom Mavis offered. A kind of best friend bandage. Mavis was known for her balanced lectures on husbands in their natural habitat. Her fifteen-year marriage to her high school beau was all the advanced degree she needed to stand at the podium of love.

"Exactly, Mavis. That is exactly right." Her mother's voice floated back to Maggie. "There's nothing to do, is there? You have to do the best with what you have. Convince everyone you're happy and you will convince yourself."

Convince yourself you're happy. *Well, that's one strategy*, she thought.

## *Free Ticket to Life*

"You're not thinking of going tonight, are you?" Big Steven was sitting on the edge of the bed in his plaid boxer shorts, pulling on his socks. "Julia?"

"Those don't match, Steven. Take them off. There's a pair here in the laundry basket." Julia upended the freshly washed clothing onto the unmade bed and rifled through the boys' tie-dyed T-shirts and cargo shorts. "You want a pair of Bob the Builder socks? The women at the office might find them hot in a sensitive man kind of way."

"You're not considering going to Maggie's tonight, are you?"

"I told her I wasn't. Can you pick up Mikey after swimming today? I've got to get to the grocery store. You'd be surprised how little you can make with yellow mustard and string cheese."

"So does that mean you aren't going?"

Julia sighed, lifted a navy bath towel, and snapped the wrinkles out. "I don't want to go, but I feel like I should support her."

Shaking his head, Steven stood and reached for his khakis. Balancing carefully, he slipped the pants on his extended leg. "I think the less time you spend with her, the less chance of getting caught up in her vortex."

She eyed his clothing choice. "You might consider using something other than the dryer to de-wrinkle your clothes. We've progressed since hot rocks. There is this thing called an iron, you know."

"What time is the meeting?"

Julia walked around to stand by her husband and squinted at his head. "Are you putting gel in your hair? It's beginning to look like a dorsal fin. Maybe it's time to go the Mr. Clean route." Julia reached up to kiss him on the ear.

"Stop flittering around. I'm not going to quit talking about this."

Julia searched for another topic to talk about. Finding nothing compelling enough to derail her husband, she said, "To be honest, I thought you'd like the idea of a Neighborhood Watch. When you *are* home, you're always bitching about the people on our street. Why not do some public bitching for a change?"

Steven straightened, buttoned the cuff of his white shirt, and said, "I've got no problem with the Neighborhood Watch. I'm fine with that. Sign us up. I just wish Maggie wasn't in charge of it."

Julie stopped making the bed and stared at her husband like he'd just asked for a threesome with a high school cheerleader. "What? It's not the Find-the-Felon Hoedown you're having trouble with? Your problem is entirely with Maggie?"

"You did fine for several years without her. I don't remember her being much help when Little Steven had meningitis or when you were pregnant and on bed rest."

"Yeah, well, she and I sometimes lost touch. That was as much my fault as hers."

"Maybe reuniting wasn't the best idea for you two."

"Yes, but she's home now. I can't just ignore her."

"She could never accuse you of ignoring her. She's been home, what, a year and a half? And she's all I ever hear about."

"So you're saying I should really focus on dry-cleaning pickup, soccer, and meal after meal after pain-in-the-ass meal? Is that it? No friends for Julia. She's got a full-time family." She widened her eyes with an I-dare-you challenge. "Did you know that Little Steven will eat only white food and Mikey is on day thirty-seven of letting only peanut butter and kiwi touch his lips? While this is riveting family entertainment, sometimes I need more."

"You can go back to work if you like. You know I won't stop you."

"I should get a job so that I don't hang out with Maggie. Seriously, Steven, tell me you aren't saying that. She's my best, longest friend."

"And she also happens to be a pain in the ass."

"She's an acquired taste. But you have to remember—she's had a tough life. Her dad was an unreliable drunk, and it hasn't been that long since she lost the baby."

"You didn't exactly get a free ticket to life, either. A dead mom at six and a cold fish for a father."

"You didn't see Maggie, Steven. You didn't see her after the baby died. I know I didn't talk about it much. It just hit too close to home. She went into the hospital on her due date. Just for a final check. The baby had died sometime in the night and she didn't know it. She went home, started labor and delivered it within twelve hours. Whenever I think of it, I see Little Steven and how sad he looked when he was in the hospital. Like a crumpled-up piece of pale paper."

Her husband ran his hand over his head and held the back of his neck.

"Afterward she held that little girl like she was fine.

She wanted pictures taken. She screamed when they came to take Ella to the morgue. Martin had to hold her, and she shoved him so hard he fell and hit his head against the windowsill. She begged to be there when they did aftercare. She said it was her right as Ella's mother. You know what? Everything she said was exactly right, given the circumstances. She deserves a little hysteria in her life. I didn't let her go it alone then, and I'm not going to now, either."

Big Steven looked down at his wife and took her hands. "Go if you want. It's up to you. You're a big girl, sassy as you are. If it means that much to you, go."

Sniffing, Julia said quietly, "Oh for Christ's sake, I was never going to go. But I sure as shit wasn't going to have you tell me I couldn't."

## *The Neighborhood Watch*

"Um, well, I guess you can never have too much safety," Maggie said, letting out a nervous laugh, while tugging at her hair and staring into the middle of the group, studiously avoiding eye contact with anyone. "In conclusion, between the calling tree, email sign-up, and rotating shift schedule, I think we can create a net of safety and herald a new era of safety and security for our families' safety." Maggie stood to the left of the buffet table and looked up from her notes, realizing she'd probably overused the word *safety*. A blond, sunburned woman yawned. Maggie saw Martin in the corner with sympathetic eyebrows and a tiny shoulder shrug that said, *Well, you tried, now let's forget about all this nonsense.*

"Before we eat, I have a few final announcements to make," Maggie said, remembering Beverly Finker's letter.

"Um, maybe some of you know Beverly Finker. She couldn't make this meeting but asked that we address some of her concerns." Opening the letter for the first time, she saw that Beverly had made a list. Maggie swallowed and read in a clear, spelling-bee voice: "Major concerns: dog feces pickup, timely trashcan retrieval, overwatering of lawns, unsightly perennials, and the meth lab on the corner of Second and Lincoln Street."

There was a murmur in the center of the group and a muffled giggle. Maggie cleared her throat and went on. "I'd like to talk about something else I've recently discovered." She felt a familiar tightening and a pricking in her nostrils and thought, *Not tears. Not in front of these people.* The blond-haired woman looked at her watch.

"I have a question," interrupted Clara Parkington, a blowsy woman in open-toed sandals and bifocals. "I notice, dear, that you have me scheduled for two 9 p.m. to 3 a.m. shifts, yet you yourself have only one 'night shift,' as it were." Clara tried to make quotation marks in the air when she spoke the words *night shift*, but she was clasping her pug, Tennessee Williams, and a plastic wineglass, so the effect was arthritic instead of astute. "Is there a reason for this?"

Maggie blinked at the intrusion and said, "That's true,

Mrs. Parkington, everyone who RSVP'd by email was given two partial nighttime shifts a month except me. I was hoping, because of my pregnancy and the organizing I've been doing, that it would be a fair trade-off."

"Well, I need my rest as much as anyone, and as it is, my sleep does not go uninterrupted. People are always overestimating the size of a pug's bladder. Besides, my Tennessee Williams is having teething troubles. I haven't had a good night's sleep since his molars came in, and a rawhide bone just isn't cutting it these days. He wants his mommy." She said this while stroking Mr. Williams under his chin. He stared with disgruntled emphasis at Maggie. "So, pregnancy or no, I believe Tennessee allows me some grace."

Maggie started to respond when Elizabeth Doody spoke up.

"Since I turned eighty-five, my sleep is frequently disrupted by my pug-like bladder, so I don't mind an extra shift or two. I'll take Clara's shift." She winked affectionately at Maggie, adding, "It's good to have you back in town."

"So, are we, like, supposed to sit up through the whole shift and, like, watch out the window for suspicious characters?"

Maggie scanned the room to locate the speaker. The voice appeared to come from a man in thick leather sandals, neutral-colored droopy clothing, and a thin patch of beard beneath his lower lip.

"Well, no. I don't expect you all to sit at your windows with a musket and a lantern." A nervous, humorless laugh escaped from Maggie's throat. She looked at the papers in her hands, felt tears collect in the corners of her eyes. Her upper lip stiffened. "I just . . . I don't know what I was thinking. Clearly you . . ."

"No, of course not." Like the audience at a tennis match, the group turned in unison to the opposite corner of the room where Martin spoke. "When your time slot comes up, you become the contact person for the neighborhood. If something happens, people are to get in touch with you and you are the support person. Then maybe you call us or the police. No one expects you to stand guard." He smiled his genial smile and said, "Now, who wants a beer?"

Martin, unruffled by the twenty-five unknown faces in his living room, chatted easily with their guests while Maggie busied herself at the buffet and glanced around surreptitiously. Previously unnamed faces seen from across fences now occupied space next to her well-loved personal treasures. Her antique lamp with the fringed creamy shade stood dignified and outraged next to a woman furtively checking the bottoms of Maggie's porcelain figurines. Her grandparents stared with puzzlement out of their mahogany picture frame at a young couple struggling to identify the hummus on the buffet. The ancient, inherited rocker in the living room held the oversized rump of a man she had earlier thought was a pear-shaped woman with very short hair. Thank goodness she wasn't a chair. All that unpredictable intimacy would be too much to bear.

Before the party began, Maggie and Martin created a complicated array of signals that could communicate everything from "fill the nut bowl" to "I'm having a panic attack." Unfortunately, Martin was so engrossed in a conversation about mulch with the large-butted man that Maggie had to walk the length of the room to grab his arm and pull him into the bathroom, where she whispered: "These people are sucking the air right out of the room."

Unsurprised, Martin said, "You're exaggerating. You're just giving in to your social anxiety."

"I don't like my neighbors. Apparently a common goal of homeland security does not make for common decency. That hairy-necked man poured his punch into my hibiscus."

Martin looked at Maggie's face, pale with anxiety, and said gently, "Honey, this was your idea, and if nothing else, it's worked out as a fine way to meet our neighbors."

"If only my mom or Julia had come." With a fierce look that was all her own she said through gritted teeth, "God, they are obstinate women."

Martin opened his mouth and started to speak, then stopped and touched his wife's chin. "So this will be the last meeting, then."

"No," Maggie said with a force that surprised her.

"Look, if it's causing you anxiety, you should get out. That's all I'm saying."

"Really? Because *you* are causing me anxiety. Should I leave you?"

Shaking his head, obviously angry, Martin said, "That was *me* in there, rescuing you, remember? Look, I'm going back to talk to that guy about mulch. Hang in there and we'll reevaluate later." Martin moved away without a backward glance and Maggie was left feeling mean and stupid. Was it the pregnancy hormones? Why wasn't she giving her husband the benefit of the doubt these days?

She walked into the kitchen and decided to lose herself in the dishes but the first plate she picked up, a white porcelain one, slipped out of her hand and broke into pieces in the metal sink.

"Shit." Maggie reached in and grasped a jagged edge, cutting the fleshy part of her palm. She jerked her hand back and stared at the cut. A white, glossy shard was imbedded in the skin, the blood beading around the slice.

She dropped her other hand to the countertop, steadying herself.

"You're looking a little wobbly there."

Startled, Maggie turned to look at the man who spoke. But the movement took away her equilibrium and she stumbled.

"Whoa. Here, let's sit you down."

He pulled a kitchen chair behind Maggie's knees and gently steered her to sit.

Maggie grasped the injured hand at the wrist and without grace sat where she was directed.

"I cut myself," she said. "Obviously." She gestured to the wedge of porcelain that sat like a minuscule shark fin in the plane of her hand.

"Let me take a look." The stranger sat down on his haunches and squinted. "I'll get that," he said, and plucked the shard out of her hand. She was looking at the black hair on the top of his head when he lifted his chin and met her eyes. He was close to her face and she could smell mint. "You should maybe have that looked at."

Standing, he dropped the glass onto the counter and unrolled a wad of paper towels.

"I'm bleeding on you."

He took her hand again, tilted it, and blotted the gash. "This is actually pretty deep." Gently he asked, "Are you okay?"

She felt the catch in her throat, the constricting she often felt when she was the recipient of kindness. Pushing against her feet, she slid her chair back and nodded, swallowing. He dropped her hand, leaving her with the paper towel. The sounds of conversation from the living room rushed back into the room, where moments before they had been pushed out.

He cleared his throat and said, "That's quite a schedule you worked out."

She checked for mockery but nothing like that seemed to rest in his eyes or in his friendly smile. "Thanks. I actually worked on it for quite a while before tonight's meeting."

"I can tell you did. It's very thorough."

Maggie flushed with the compliment. "I was always good at spatial relationships and logical reasoning, a total right brainer." She used her uninjured hand to bolster herself up to a standing position.

"I don't know. The food has definite lefty qualities. I like how you carved the zucchini into a trough for the dip."

"A boat." She dabbed at her hand.

"Pardon?"

"The zucchini is a boat and those are celery oars next to it." And then she added with a grin and a shrug, "A trough sounds too piggy."

"It's no wonder I didn't recognize it. I'm not accustomed to looking for seacraft on a buffet."

Maggie's shoulders dropped an inch and the people at the party seemed to recede again. "To be honest, this is the first time I tried to sculpt vegetables. I saw it in a magazine, but it's harder than it looks," Maggie said, and then added, "It's not really worth the time."

"Good to know."

She looked into his face and laughed at herself. "I think you may be the only one impressed with the food or the scheduling system."

"I don't think that's true. I think people want to be organized; they just don't want to know the specifics. Or maybe they only like organization as a concept."

"I had more exciting agenda topics, but I got interrupted and then I lost my nerve. This whole meeting is a little out of character for me. Losing my nerve is the only thing I did that was *in* character."

"Is that right?" He was looking at her, interested and curious.

"I hate public speaking. Once, for show-and-tell in kindergarten I told the class that my dad would be running for president of the United States. He had taken a trip to DC and had a hundred-dollar bill in his wallet. I knew the president lived in Washington, and I guess I confused the presence of money for having a job." She shrugged. "I've been gun-shy ever since."

"You did fine tonight. I'm David Johnson. I live in the neighborhood. You and your husband have a very nice home here. When is the baby due?"

"Nice to meet you, David." Maggie held out her hand. His grip was warm. He actually shook her hand like it was a real greeting. Sincere. So many handshakes with men said, *You're a woman and we will never be friends because you are not my equal, so I can only give you the weakest of welcomes.* "Seven weeks. I have some time yet."

"Wow, you don't look that far along. Are you ready? All my friends who have children say it's quite an adjustment. Once you have one, there's no going back."

"I don't think you're ever really ready." Maggie looked into his eyes and said, "We lost our first child."

"My God," he murmured. "I am so sorry. I am a total idiot."

"No, it's okay," and she reached to touch him, stopping just short of his shoulder. "I don't know why I told you that. Must be the non-alcoholic wine, the bubbles or something." She shrugged to quiet the obvious unease they both felt.

*Oh, Lord,* she thought. *Why am I still talking?*

He looked at her closely and said, "This is why I don't go out much. I'm conversationally impaired. I can do interested and occasionally benign, but often I blunder into insensitivity or get overly personal. Then once I'm in, I can't seem to back out, and the next thing you know I'm talking nonstop and asking about the brand of your underwear."

"Jockey," Maggie said with a self-conscious grin.

"What?"

"Jockey, I wear Jockey. Unless it's a special occasion like Lent or, say, movie night, then I try to find my Calvin Klein's. But typically they are buried so far down in the drawer I just have to be happy with the Jockeys. These days, though, I could wear my grandmother's grundies and be thrilled."

When he laughed, Maggie noticed a slightly crooked tooth right in the center that seemed to say, *This man is a nice man. It's okay to be comfortable*. He had short black hair with strands of gray in his sideburns, but he was young, probably younger than she was. She had to look up just slightly to see his whole face and she wondered if he was taller than Martin. There was a curling of chest hair at the top of his white T-shirt, which he wore under a white button-down cotton shirt. He had the blunt fingers Maggie associated with a mechanic, but his nails were short and clean.

Reaching to touch his forearm, she whispered, "Maybe you shouldn't tell the rest of the Neighborhood Watch my underwear style, or anything else, if that's okay."

"Your secrets are safe with me."

"Well, I hope I can reciprocate." And then with an awkward pause she added, "I mean keeping a secret some time." And she smiled again and looked away, embarrassed.

"I'm sorry to hear about your first child." He looked directly at her with beautiful empathy. As beautiful and surprising as northern lights on the horizon.

"I'm sorry I mentioned it. It's a conversation killer."

The overhead light in the kitchen blinked, sputtered, and went out. "Crap," Maggie said. "This is constantly happening. I think the light has some sort of distress meter and when awkwardness is at an all-time high, it shuts off, probably hoping the room will clear."

David looked intently up at the light fixture. "How often does this happen?"

"Oh, whenever I'm in here, which is several times a day. The problem is that we don't know a thing about electricity and since we're sort of new to the area, we don't know who to call, or who can be trusted with the repair."

David hesitated for just a second and said, "I'm pretty good at this kind of thing. Give me a call if you're interested, and I'll see if I can figure it out. I work at home, so whenever it's convenient for you." He picked up a pen lying on the counter and asked for a piece of paper to write down his number. Maggie reached for the pad by the phone.

"This is great, thank you. We really don't deserve to own a home. The only projects we can complete are ones that can be solved with a butter knife, and those are surprisingly few." She watched him write his name and asked, "What do you do?"

"I'm a freelance writer. I specialize in travel pieces and home renovation. My dad died last year, and I moved home to live with my mom to help her out. She's lonely. My fiancée is teaching a writing course in France for a year, so it worked out well." He pulled the top sheet off the pad and handed it to Maggie.

"Unless you've decided to schedule me for more weekends, I think I'll head out," he said. "I've talked to all the interesting people here tonight."

*Don't go. Don't leave me here with the others,* she thought. Instead she said, "I probably will call you, if you don't mind," as he walked out the door and waved. Maggie tucked the paper into her waistband and walked straight back into the living room.

Like people tethered together on a belay line, the movement of one pulled the rest from the room. Within an hour, the people were gone, the kitchen sink was cleared, her hand was properly bandaged, and the dishwasher was loaded. Maggie could hear Martin downstairs getting ready to run on the treadmill, his typical post-party purge, and Maggie sank into the rocking chair, reclaiming her space. She replayed her announcements of the evening and tried to put some faces and names together for future interactions. The light in the kitchen flickered back on and she remembered the paper tucked into her waistband, and unwound the gauze around her hand.

Eyeing the cut on her hand, now the color of rust, she stood, walked to the front picture window, and pulled out the note to read the name and phone number of the guy with whom she'd had the most engaging conversation of the evening. Glancing up and outside, she noticed a dark gray van parked across the street in front of her house. Seated behind the wheel was a man whose face she could not clearly see. She made out the outline of glasses and some facial hair as he looked down to start his car. He turned his head her way and drove off.

*Oh my God,* she thought. *That's him.*

## *A Sure Thing*

"Maggie, wake up."

Maggie opened her eyes and immediately saw Martin's face a few inches away, squinting at her with far-sighted concern. "You're having a nightmare."

She jolted awake and pushed her hair, damp with sweat, away from her face. "Oh, God. I was trying to wake myself."

Martin propped himself against the headboard. Easing Maggie in his direction, he coaxed her head to his chest, smoothing her hair away from her forehead. With his free hand, he scratched her back. He yawned. "Was it the dream where you're trying to dial 9-1-1?"

Slightly out of breath, she said, "No. It's the one where

I forgot the baby at home while I was at the grocery store. I tried to get to her, but I couldn't find my keys and the car tires were flat. I've had this dream before, but this time that guy—Tyson, the online perv—was walking toward our house. I tried to run. I couldn't move my legs and I couldn't yell." She shuddered.

Martin bent forward and kissed the clean part in her hair, and Maggie pulled the sheet up higher under her chin. "What a monumental relief, just a dream." She closed her eyes. "You know, I checked an online Internet dream interpretation service last week, looking for an analysis."

"What'd it say?"

"Nothing I didn't already know. That my nightmare symbolizes fear, powerlessness, and insecurity."

"Sounds to me like you need to stay away from the Internet in general. It's not very supportive of you."

"Maybe you're right," she sighed. "Maybe I should go back to counseling."

It was a warm night and she could hear the wind and the trees mimicking the sound of rain for an audience of katydids. Nature's comic impersonations of nature, something to occupy the time when people-watching wasn't possible. When all the interesting ones were asleep inside their homes.

Maggie shifted her weight and turned onto her back.

Martin placed his hand on her belly. She said, "You're nice."

"Thank you." He outlined her chin with his fingers.

"Do you remember when you asked me out?" she asked.

"Of course I do."

"Julia wasn't impressed when I came home to say that the *intern* at the help desk had asked me out."

"I'm outraged. Bill Gates was probably an intern at some university somewhere, once upon a time."

"Touché," she said with a breathy laugh. "After she met you, she liked you, though. She said you were calm."

He closed his eyes briefly and rubbed the lids with his thumb and forefinger. "What did *you* like? Was it my quick wit and generally snazzy wardrobe?"

"Buddy, you needed a good haircut and a shirt without *Royall High School* printed on it before you could spell *snazzy*."

"Then what was it that you liked, smarty pants?"

"You were kind. Kindness is the umbrella that covers honesty, integrity, and character. If you have kindness, you have the trifecta."

"You make me sound like a racehorse." His hand inched under her pajama top and started making its way upward. "I'll be a racehorse if I get to be the stud," and he raised his eyebrows in proposition.

An instant pained expression crossed Maggie's face. "C'mon, Martin."

"I'd be a quick stud. I'd even let you bridle me." His hand was on her breast and he was moving to kiss her.

"Yeah, that's exactly what women want, quick sex with a muzzle." Rolling away from his touch, she said, "Why do you always do that? We're having a nice conversation, engaging in a little nostalgia, and the next thing I know it's the backseat at the high school dance."

"Except we're married, and people have sex when they're married."

"We have sex. If we didn't, I wouldn't be spending all my time shopping for elastic-top jeans."

"That was more than six months ago."

"Oh, come off it. We've had sex since I've been pregnant."

Martin didn't speak. He flounced onto his back and tried to pull the covers up. "I'm going back to sleep."

"All I'm saying is, have you ever seen a romantic movie where the leading man grabs the starlet's boob and hot sex ensues? A girl likes a little romance. A little warning."

"More like an engraved invitation. I get it. Dinner and a movie followed by a backrub and Martin gets laid. If I'm lucky. Forget it."

Sitting back on her heels, Maggie said, "You may be kind at times, but other times you are an ass. Pardon me for not putting out in the middle of the night after a stressful dream."

When he didn't respond, she pushed herself off the bed. "I get it now. I'm only interesting enough to talk to if there will be payoff sex. Fine. Go to sleep."

Out of bed now, she fumbled around for her slippers, stalked out of the room, and headed down the stairs to the kitchen. The backs of her slippers slapped at her heels, a disgruntled, halfhearted disciplinary action for getting out of bed. Maggie touched her belly and willed her child to jiggle a little, to make her little life known. She wanted ice-cold water. She had learned during her prenatal doctor's visits that drinking cold water got the baby to move around. She drank a lot of cold water during this pregnancy just to feel the reassuring tumble of elbows and knees inside of her. It must be irritating for the child to be woken as often as Maggie sipped, but she would let the child sleep undisturbed once she was out and safely in her arms.

In the kitchen, she opened the fridge, a bad habit like smoking while on the phone or eating in the car. A visit to the kitchen was not a visit to the kitchen unless a refrigerator was opened. Anxiety was not anxiety unless the oven was checked for a flame, the bathroom rug was straightened, and all facial pores were examined for blemishes.

Sipping cold water straight from the pitcher, she

walked to the back door. Unlatching the lock and stepping onto the stoop, she stood there in the darkness, as a breeze gently lifted her hair. The sounds of the night were pleasurable and familiar. Her wakefulness often brought her outside, hoping the summer air would wash the old weblike worries from her mind. Her wristwatch read 3 a.m. A streetlight flickered.

Without actually making a conscious decision to move, Maggie started down the back steps and headed toward her bicycle, which leaned against the garage. *It's time for some action, Mr. C. Tyson*, she thought. She bent, picked up the rose clippers, and dropped them into her blue-and-white basket, a throwback to a simpler time when bikes were used to make flower deliveries and to carry newspapers and groceries. Maybe a baguette, if in France. She wasn't in France, though. She was on Hemlock Street, in Elmwood, Wisconsin, a street dressed up like Norman Rockwell but with Norman Bates potential.

Kicking off with her slippered foot, Maggie coasted down her driveway on the bicycle, riding on one pedal like a pregnant circus girl on a pony. With confidence, she swung her leg around, leveraging her belly for balance, and mounted her steed. She was a showgirl, a tomboy, a sure thing.

In her lavender waffle-weave pajamas with the satin piping and covered buttons, she pumped the pedals down

Hemlock Street, knowing full well that Mrs. Peketti was on watch tonight. Everyone talked about Mrs. Peketti like she was Mr. Bojangles: *She drinks a bit.* Maggie felt strong on her bike and soundlessly peddled toward her destination. The baby kicked in delight.

She slowed at Tyson's house and swung her leg off her bike. Steering with one hand and supporting her belly with the other, she landed quietly. There were two beautiful, potted red geraniums sitting like bookends on the asphalt, creating a gated look to the driveway. Gorgeous lush heads strained upward, searching for a sun long gone to sleep. Without looking around, Maggie bent to smell the spicy floral scent that reminded her of May, Mother's Day, and spring.

Then, reaching into her basket, she steadily and efficiently clipped the new, beautiful craniums off each and every green leafy stalk until a puddle of redheaded blooms collected at her lavender-shod feet. She studied her work, turned, dropped her clippers into her basket, and jumped back on her bike.

Back in her bedroom, Maggie tiptoed across the wood floor, navigating carefully around the squeaks that would give her away. With her arms encircling her midsection, she moved silently toward the bed. Then she knocked her shin into the forgotten laundry basket sitting right at its foot. She caught her breath and froze. Martin repositioned himself, pulled the covers across his body, and mumbled. "C'mon back to bed. I don't want to fight."

Easing herself down, her heart pounding, she rolled on her side and held her breath. Martin rotated slightly and pulled her close, entwining his legs with hers. His voice was filled with a quiet, muffled apology. "Your feet are freezing. Where'd you go?"

"Nowhere. Just downstairs for a drink of water."

"What time is it?"

"No idea, sweetie. Go to sleep."

With her face alert and her eyes wide, Maggie snuggled down and waited for Martin's regular breathing, his telltale snore. Looking around their room, feeling the wet hem of her pajamas against her shin, she once again considered the dream interpretation. She wondered what it was that people dreamed about when they felt powerful and decisive and in control of their lives. *Maybe nothing at all.*

## *A Chocolate-Cake Decision*

Maggie couldn't remember the last time she'd felt this happy first thing in the morning. Simple, sunny-yellow happiness without the typical marbling of apprehension or anxiety woven in. She had forgotten this sensation, misplaced it within the recesses of her brain, like dust underneath the couch cushions.

Sitting on her unmade bed, she leaned forward to tie her running shoes. For once she understood a phrase her mother used to use when she was a kid, sometimes to help justify a shopping trip or an impromptu dinner out. "It is a chocolate-cake decision," her mother would say. She would wear her flirty sideways grin and explain, "A chocolate-cake decision is one where you know something is absolutely unnecessary and maybe a poor choice, but the decision to partake of it is rooted in only one question: Will it taste good?" Maggie remembered the collection of velvety red petals at her feet the night before, the still air, the feeling inside her when blade met botany. *Oh, yes, and yes again, it did taste good*, she thought.

Outside, dressed for exercise, Maggie hurried toward Julia's house, her legs feeling stronger with every stride. She spotted Julia up ahead on the straight sidewalk, waved, and jogged to greet her. Reaching a hand to support her belly, which pushed out gently against her windbreaker, she called, "Morning!"

"Hey!" Julia said. "I'm glad you phoned. I needed to get my rear end out of the house today. Even though it looks like rain, I can't stay in and clean pubic hair out of my shower drain again. We're knee-deep; we're a hair factory; we are an overstock hair surplus store and everything must go."

"You're disgusting." The two women moved together and paced their strides equally.

"You know it's true. You've been in my bathroom."

"Why don't you hire a cleaning lady? You can afford it."

"I can't bring myself to do it. When I was working, I paid half of what a cleaning lady charges per hour for daycare. If I pay what they are asking, I'm essentially saying that wiping grime off the stove is worth more than caring for my kids."

Maggie shook her head. "No, you're just saying, here's some money, wipe the grime off my stove."

"It's a philosophical issue. Besides, talk about a bad investment. Within a half hour of my paying a hundred bucks to clean the dried pee off the toilet, Little Steven will come home and re-pee. I may as well leave the original pee for a week or two and, boom, instant college savings plan."

"Honestly, whose mind works like that?"

"Honestly, mine does." Julia glanced at Maggie. "Why are you looking so perky and what's with the late exercise program?" The women turned into the Elmwood High School parking lot—home of the Gladiators—and crossed onto County Road B.

"I was exhausted after last night's Neighborhood Watch meeting, so I slept in. I still wanted to get some exercise outside. It's so beautiful today."

Julia eyed her friend. "I think it's supposed to rain—" Then she broke off. "Did you get laid, is that it?"

"God, you and Martin both. Can't a girl be happy without sex being involved? I just feel like moving, and I know I won't feel like that for long. I'm getting bigger every day."

Julia let out an exasperated sigh. "Perfect and prettily

pregnant is all you'll ever know. I, on the other hand, was a swollen hormone heap with varicose veins and a pregnancy mask."

"That may be, but you look amazing now."

"Listen, I was in such a hormone storm I became the bearded lady of Columbus County overnight. My facial hair was thick and completely resistant to all methods of removal. NASA should have made their space shuttle with that hair. It easily could have withstood reentry into our atmosphere without singeing a follicle."

"You're in rare form today," Maggie said with a smile.

"I'm just pissy because I'm late this month and I'm sweating it."

"You're late? Really? How late?" Maggie widened her eyes and brushed at a collection of gnats mysteriously clustered and suspended in the air.

"Late enough that if my mother-in-law finds out, she'll put me in the prayer box at church. If those old ladies get ahold of me, what started as premenopause will turn into a fertilized baby in no time."

Maggie elbowed Julia playfully. "Hasn't anyone given you the condom talk?"

"As I remember it, I gave *you* the condom talk. I seriously don't know how it happened. I'm on the pill, and I'm usually very good about taking it. But you know what they say, 'usually' makes an ass out of u and me."

"Isn't that 'assume'?"

"Just shut up," Julia said. She picked up her pace and turned to look at Maggie. "I don't want to talk about it," she added. "Tell me about the creepy watcher's party."

"So, that's how it is. You want nothing to do with the Neighborhood Watch, but you aren't opposed to collecting stories on your neighbors and reaping safety benefits."

"What's wrong with that? I'm giving you my full attention and support while simultaneously creating the perfect workout environment. I'm your personal trainer slash behind-the-scenes consultant."

"I'd prefer your help front and center."

"Look, it's not like I don't think your idea has merit, especially given your recent discovery. I'm just not sure I want to grant my neighbors free license to peer through their dining room sheers to spy on the rest of us. Besides, you know I have terrible insomnia. Sometimes I shut off the sprinklers in the middle of the night in a T-shirt that barely covers my ass. I want to be slovenly and forgetful without a scheduled viewing audience, and the Neighborhood Watch makes me feel like I'm always one false move away from the slammer."

"Your sleep disorder makes you perfect for the Watch. You could take the midnight shifts and get Clara Parkington and her pug off my back."

"You scheduled a pug? You are desperate. Still, no way.

I put that time to good use working out life's mysteries. Like for instance, have you ever wondered why women are programmed to love what will ultimately do them in: butter, men, and time?" Julia swiped the sweat off her forehead.

"Couldn't you contemplate life's mysteries in front of your picture window with a notebook and be both a deep thinker *and* a crime fighter?"

"I don't just sit around and ponder. I like to roam the house, walk outside, pull weeds, tighten the bolts on light fixtures, or just lie in the grass and stare at the moon. If I can persuade Big Steven to get out of bed, I like to make love under the slide in the backyard and talk about the future. I don't want nosey Mrs. Belchner to haul her doughy husband to the window to discuss our uncreative technique. Screwing with a headless Power Ranger at my shoulder and a plastic shovel digging into my back makes me feel real."

With her silence, Maggie agreed to allow Julia her eccentricities. *Lord knows I have my own,* thought Maggie. The cloud cover created a kind of muffled quiet in the neighborhood.

"I wish you had been there," said Maggie. "It was horrible, actually. Well, not entirely horrible. I was able to make my announcements and get the schedule out to everyone, but they were all so . . . typical."

"Well, this is small-town America, honey, what did you expect? The *New York Times* art critic?"

"No, I just didn't think they'd all be so irritating."

"I told you not to expect too much—they came for the food."

"Martin had a conversation with the man who has the gorgeous garden on Maple. You know the one with all the lawn art and bird feeders?"

"You mean the woman with the butch hair cut?"

"He's a man. He just has a really unfortunate fat distribution," Maggie said charitably. Julia laughed her big laugh and shook her head.

"Hey, what'd ya do to your hand?" asked Julia.

"Stupid. I broke a plate and cut myself. But that reminds me, I did have one good chat," she said. She pulled off her sun visor and replaced it more firmly on her head to shield her eyes. "It was a quick one, about nothing, really. He asked me when I was due, said he was good at fixing things."

"Yeah?" Julia asked.

"He was there when I cut my hand. We didn't talk that long. He moved here to help his mother after his father died. I think he's only been back for a short time. He's got a fiancée in France."

"Good girl! You actually found out a lot of intel in a short time. Where's he live?"

Maggie shrugged. "I don't know. His name is David Johnson. He was nice. Cute and funny, too."

Julia turned to look at Maggie. "Now we're getting somewhere."

"I'm just saying he wasn't your usual 'How 'bout those Packers?' kind of guy. You should come to the next meeting to check him out."

"If you want to make hors d'oeuvres for a bunch of frustrated cop wannabes, knock yourself out. I don't want to go to those meetings. I'll eat my hummus at home with my own obsessions, thank you."

They had come full circle and Maggie tried to fasten her face into an expression of calm interest as they approached Tyson's house. But her face flushed and she pulled her visor down to cover her eyes. After a few moments, she touched Julia on the arm and with careful nonchalance said, "Hey, look where we are."

Julia grasped Maggie's sleeve. "You're not going to throw yourself on his porch, are you?"

Maggie laughed awkwardly. "No, not today."

"I used to love this house before you told me who lives in it. It's so charming. And look at all the flowers. These will be pretty when they bloom." Julia bent to touch the headless geraniums sitting at the end of the driveway.

Maggie looked at the plants. Someone had cleaned up the carnage, and the innocent-looking plants sat blind and staring, naked as newly shorn sheep. Maggie turned, sped up her pace, and pulled Julia by the arm. Moving away from the house, she said, "Come on, I don't want him to think I'm stalking him."

"Well, you are kind of keeping an eye on him."

"I know that, but I don't want *him* to know that. Geez, don't you ever watch any television?"

"I've watched enough cable to be able to waive forensic school, girlie, but I have to break it to you. We are not on TV here."

"One other thing happened last night," Maggie said looking at her friend.

Julia raised her eyebrows and waited.

"After everyone left, there was one of those big windowless vans parked outside my house. There was a guy sitting in it."

"A guy? What guy? Was it the pevert?"

"I don't know. I really couldn't see."

"What did Martin say? Did you call the cops?"

"No, the van drove away right after I saw him. I didn't tell Martin. He would think I was just creating drama because I want to keep the Watch going."

Julia shook her head. "I don't want to talk about this anymore."

Maggie was quiet and sighed. "Okay, let's talk about something easy. Tell me about Little Steven's day camp."

The two women moved away, circling back to their neighborhood and heading toward the rest of their day. At her front door Maggie watched Julia walk away. Her blond ponytail was shining in the sunlight. Maggie took a minute to sit quietly on the steps. Breathing deeply, she exhaled and placed her hands on her mound of belly, which rested like an egg on the nest of her upper thighs. She felt her baby moving. *I can do this,* she thought. "All of it. With or without Julia. I can build a moat, create a trench of safety. I can," she whispered to herself and her child.

# *A Hard Day Is Not a Bad Day*

Julia walked the rest of the way home quickly. She moved up her driveway and into her side yard, stepping around a yellow plastic dump truck and half of a Batman dressed in an evening gown. She kicked a lopsided soccer ball out of her way and sat on one of the swings suspended under the wooden play structure. She sighed. The dandelions had won this year, same as last.

She stared in surprise and curiosity as Big Steven drove up in the Hybrid they purchased last year. The passenger side window automatically receded and Steven called, "Hey, Sexy, come here often?"

Matching his volume, Julia laughed. "Well, Sailor, it

depends who's asking. Don't think you can just show up every once in a great while and sweet-talk a girl. There's some deck swabbing to do."

He stepped out of the car and walked to where his wife sat.

"Pull up a swing," she said. "What're you doing home?"

Steven bent and sat on the plastic rocking horse suspended from the overhead beam. "I came to pack a bag. I've got a fund-raiser in Minneapolis I have to go to. Where are the boys?"

Julia shook her head with irritation. "I don't know how you *don't* know that Little Steven is at day camp and Mikey swims until noon. *Every day.* Could you at least pretend you keep us in mind once in a while?"

Steven pursed his lips. "Could we go back to the sailor role-play?" he asked. "We could switch to nurse and wounded war hero if you like, but the conversation we're having right now isn't as sexy as you might think."

Julia picked up a rifle-sized water pistol and whacked at a giant weed growing up the side of the swing set. "I just finished walking with Maggie."

"Oh, Maggie," Steven said knowingly.

As if to herself, Julia said, "I've seen her like this before. Not as someone who rights all wrongs but as someone who obsessively seeks a kind of perfection that doesn't exist." She gestured pointedly around her. "I always think that if you don't go looking for perfection you are far less likely to notice flaws in the tapestry."

With a puzzled look Steven said, "It seems odd, you know, given her history, that Maggie would grow up thinking *perfection* is attainable."

"Yeah. Exactly what I would think. Maybe it's because she experienced, if only briefly, a happy family unit of mother, father, daughter. You know, a glimpse of the ideal before the trouble began with her dad. Maybe I'm okay with *okay* because my normal has always been deviant."

"Just so you know, I'm not taking that personally. I'm assuming you're talking about the lawn and not me."

Julia shoved him. "Oh, shut up. Your job is to sit quietly and say, 'Really? Tell me more.' "

Steven laughed. "Okay, tell me more."

She squeezed his hand. "After my mom died when I was born, and my dad emotionally shut down, it was like he did everything a father would do but hang his hat on the peg of true emotion. I get that. He was overwhelmed. Then, when Grandma came with her working mantra—*A hard day isn't a bad day*—we just adopted that attitude. But Maggie, even after all these years, believes a good day can only be good through vigilance."

"You can't save her, Julia. You can't keep her from getting in her own way. She has to figure it out."

"I know. You can't believe how hard I'm trying not

to mother her. To shut my mouth and stay uninvolved." Julia blinked at her husband, as if she were really seeing him for the first time. "Where'd you get that shirt? That's been in the stain pile for a month. It's got grape jelly on the sleeve." Steven looked at his arm. Julia stood and the swing bobbled and jerked with freedom. "You've got to get another job. You're never around. Taking care of the boys is a never-ending job of mind-numbing repetition. Eat your fruit, stop grabbing your ding-ding, say excuse me. You should have to do some of that."

"You're right."

"I used to be a nurse. A nurse! I was smart. I wore white hose. Now, if I get out of my sweats, it's practically a formal occasion."

"You haven't started your period, have you?" Steven said with anticipation in his voice.

"Don't you dare be excited, Steven Bagley Morris the Third. If you freaking send even one ray of positive energy toward my womb, I'm going to knife you in your sleep."

"Come on, Julia. Tell me you aren't a little excited about the prospect of another child. Maybe a little girl this time."

"It could be a groundhog for all I care. I do not want to have a baby and I'm not going to think about having a baby. Shut up."

"Really? Tell me more."

"God, you are a brat shit." With uncharacteristic seriousness she looked at Steven and said, "I need help. I'm sinking. I love the boys and you, but I need you home and I need to not be pregnant."

"I think having Maggie back stresses you out."

Julia gave a shout of frustration. "You are not hearing me. Maggie's hard. Yes. But she's a hell of a lot more interesting than a macaroni sculpture. And I'll tell you something else, I know you think I keep her afloat. That's where you're dead wrong. She keeps me afloat. Now go pack your bag. I'm going to the drugstore to buy a pregnancy test."

## *Mystery Date*

Maggie settled on the title Operation Craig Tyson (OCT) for her nighttime adventures. Pulling the brown accordion file out of the heavy fire-proof security box, she wrote *OCT* on the cover—the similarity to OCD intended. Rubbing her eyes, she stacked her Neighborhood Watch notes and Beverly Finker's increasingly persistent memos into a tidy pile with her OAL (Offender Activity Ledger) and OCT notes and placed them into the safe. Maggie silently slid the heavy box into the back of her closet and began to ease the door shut.

"What are you doing on the floor?"

Maggie snapped her head around. "Martin. God, you scared me. You slink around here like a cat."

He frowned. "No, I don't."

"I was just going through my closet, trying to see what we can clear out before the baby comes."

"Did you find anything?"

Pushing herself off the floor with a little puff, Maggie tried to stand. Upright, she wobbled a little. "Oh, I'm dizzy when I stand up."

Martin reached toward her and gently touched her shoulder. He steered her to the bed. "Here, take a seat. Can I bring you a glass of water?"

"I'm fine. The vertigo comes and goes, but mostly only when I stand up."

"What were your plans for the day? I think you should take it easy."

"I have some errands to run." Hoping to avoid her husband's inevitable question—"What type of errands?"—she added quickly, "I want to work on the baby's room."

"God forbid I tell you what to do with your time, but why don't you call that guy from the party and see if he will help? Didn't you say he offered?"

"Only to fix the light in the kitchen."

"So get him over here. Maybe he's willing to do some other stuff, like paint."

Maggie chewed her lip. "Can you call him?"

"I didn't even meet him. Why can't you call him?"

"Talking to strange men is not my forte."

"I thought you said he was nice. He told you to call if you needed help, so just call him."

"I don't want him to get the wrong idea."

"For God's sake, I doubt he'll think you're hitting on him. You're eight and a half months pregnant."

Fairly sure there was an insult in his certainty, Maggie said, "What? You don't think I have any game now that I'm going to be a mother?"

"All right, I'll call him," he said, rolling his eyes.

Maggie sat on a stool during the telephone conversation and became increasingly annoyed. Martin and David chatted, easily moving from the subject of hardware to computers to softball. Martin even invited David to play on his league team. Maggie scribbled a note on a piece of paper and handed it to Martin. *Excuse me, he's my friend!* it read. After looking at it, Martin crumbled it into a ball and tossed it NBA-style into the trash, silently lifting his free arm in victory for the two-pointer.

Complete with tools and his good-neighbor face, David finished fiddling with the fuse box in the basement and started up the stairs. Standing in her kitchen, Maggie automatically smoothed her bangs on her forehead and tapped her foot. She sat and abruptly stood again.

*C'mon, get a grip. Repairmen have come into your house before. This isn't a date.* She busied herself by opening the window blinds, as if to say, *See, nothing to hide. Just one acquaintance helping another.* She caught her reflection in the window, wearing her largest maternity blouse—an oversized mess of a thing that screeched virgin birth from the pleated front panels to the tiny pink flower buds in the fabric—and grimaced. She looked like a child playing a pregnant woman.

Maggie cleared her throat. "Are you certain you have the right fuse disengaged?" she asked. "I would feel horrible if you fried in my kitchen trying to do me a favor. I've burned a roast or two, but never a whole man." Swallowing hard she added, "Not that you're a piece of meat or anything, I just . . ." She froze.

David grasped the stepladder and began to climb. He was wearing a leather tool belt over jeans and a navy T-shirt. The back of his shirt was caught up in the belt and Maggie wanted to reach up and pull it down. Her tidiness gene, as usual, working overtime.

Intent on his work, David said, "Don't worry, I'd rather not embarrass myself by singeing any body parts."

He stood in an awkward position, bent slightly back at the waist, unscrewing the light fixture while holding the glass globe that covered the bulbs. The front of his T-shirt rose slightly and she could see black hairs on his abdomen. She looked away. The serious smell of August made her feel like summer school vacation, like heading for the swimming hole and swinging on a tire swing. Maggie reached up to unstick the hairs on the back of her neck.

David was concentrating on what he was doing, and Maggie found herself feeling like she was part surgical nurse and part helpless female. Neither was a role she felt comfortable with; the first involved too many tools, the second involved none. She gazed up at him working, narrowed her eyes, and asked, "How old are you?"

David stopped working and looked sideways at her. She noticed the charming lines at the corners of his eyes. "Thirty-three," he said. "Were you thinking, how could someone so young possibly know so much about wiring?"

Maggie felt sweat pool in the center of her back, the exact place where her embarrassment lived.

"Just getting information for the paramedics," she said weakly, and David laughed. "Actually," Maggie said, "I was thinking how odd it was that we both lived here when we were younger but never knew each other."

He reached up with the cutters to strip the wire. "We moved to town in 1991. I was fourteen. When did you leave town?"

"That explains it. I left when I graduated from high school in 1990."

Julia would say he had a nice ass and Maggie decided

she would have to agree with Julia's assessment. His jeans were tight in the right places and he seemed to have no discernable belly. Martin had a runner's body without really trying. He was lean, skinny even. David had more structure, more depth. He wore running shoes and Maggie was tempted to ask if he jogged to keep in shape. She decided against this as it would imply she noticed his in-shapedness, and that was far too intimate, especially coupled with the age question. The sleeve of his T-shirt slipped up his arm and Maggie watched his biceps flex as he turned the screwdriver.

She recalled their conversation the evening of the Neighborhood Watch party. "How's your mom doing without your father?" she asked.

"She's doing surprisingly well. My dad was sick for a long time before he died. He had a stroke and was living in the front room for a year before he was transferred to a nursing home. I know she misses him, but I can see she feels freer these days. She'd never admit it, though."

"My dad died when I was twelve," Maggie said without thinking.

David stopped what he was doing and looked at her. "I'm sorry." He said it in the way a good friend says it, with meaning, and not just to fill the silence.

"Yeah, I still miss him. When I was six, he built a dollhouse for me." She paused and said again without thinking, "He was good with his hands, too." Maggie took a sip of her water. "It had a red roof and four tiny rooms. I'd forgotten all about that house."

After a moment of quiet, David said, "The last few years, I mostly kept in touch with my parents on the phone. My dad and I had a strained relationship, and since I traveled so much with my writing, it was a good excuse to stay away." He wiped a bead of sweat from his temple with his wrist. "I ultimately came home to keep my mom company. Now she really has something to worry about—her strange recluse son who sits around and writes all day." He grunted with this last sentence, exerting some pressure on the final nut holding the fixture in place.

"Can I help you?"

"Not really. Just hold the light here and I'll get to work on the connections."

Maggie reached up for the large glass globe and held it to her, resting the glass on her belly.

"What do you write?" Maggie asked.

"It depends on the day. Mostly, I write nonfiction political pieces for magazines and newspapers. Sometimes I write travel articles for *Backpacking Magazine* and *National Geographic*. Lately, I've been working on my novel."

"Really, a novel? What's it about?"

"I don't know, but when I come up with something,

you'll be the third to know. I have to tell my mom and fiancée first. Otherwise they'll be pissed."

Maggie gave him a puzzled look. There was an inside joke in the air and she was an outsider. The word *fiancée* reminded her that she was married and spoken for. That there were lives between them and the world was bigger than the room they stood in.

David stopped working for a minute and focused his eyes on her. "I don't have a novel yet per se. I have lots of ideas for one, but the characters are vague and the plot-lines messy." He lifted a shoulder, as if he were brushing his thoughts off. "I say I'm writing a novel so I can justify living with my mom and not feel like a total loser. I thought if I took some time off and lived rent free, a novel would seep out of my head." He turned back to his work, twisting the wires in the ceiling. "That's the big secret in my life; I'm a novelist without a book, a dog without a bone."

"I'm an anal-retentive without a fixation," Maggie said. Knowing this wasn't entirely true, she added, "And I'm pregnant so that I can alphabetize Dr. Seuss books and wash clothes with fabric softener."

"The perfect pair, you and I. Tom Clancy meets Martha Stewart. How's that for a reality show?"

Maggie laughed. "It would be all frosting-piped cookies and nanny cams."

She laughed again, and then, to her supreme humiliation, she snorted. Covering her nose with her hand, she said, “Have I read any of your work?”

“You just snorted.”

“It *is* my kitchen. I can snort all day long without apology.”

“Good answer,” he said nodding. “I use a pseudonym when I publish—David Patel. My publishers think I am a well-traveled, well-read Indian man who lives in Davis, California. I send all my stuff through an agent.” He climbed down from the ladder and turned to face her. He was holding a screwdriver and wire cutter, and Maggie stepped a few paces away from him to put some space between them. She felt the stove at her back and she looked up into his face. He slipped the wire cutters into his side pocket and stooped to take the electrical tape out of the red toolbox.

“So, are you always so deceptive?” she asked.

“Out of necessity, yes. My fans would storm my house if they knew where I lived.” Then, as if he were driving a car and were about to hit a speed bump, he switched lanes. “I think you should put a ceiling fan in here. It would help with the ventilation and give you more light.”

Maggie ignored his bid to change the subject. “So, will your fiancée be Mrs. David Patel?” Suddenly she didn’t want to think about his fiancée. “I never thought of a ceiling fan. That’s a good idea.”

He said, "They're good for clearing the air."

Suddenly, Maggie realized that she wanted both to avoid the reality of David's fiancée and to satisfy her curiosity. The struggle between avoidance and knowledge proved too great. "Where in France is your fiancée?" she finally asked.

"Right in Paris. She teaches in a study-abroad program. It's a nice deal all around; they get a flexible instructor and she gets to satisfy her wanderlust."

"Do you miss her?" Alarmed by her own question, she added, "Of course you do. That was a weird question for me to ask."

David stopped putting his tools away and glanced at Maggie. "Do you miss Martin when he's gone?"

"I suppose. I mean, yes, of course. But sometimes it's nice to get a break. You know, to chew your cuticles without a spectator."

He looked at her and admitted, "Sometimes I wonder if I'm going to be any good at marriage because I like that a little too much." He glanced up at the light fixture and added, "I'm a bit of a loner."

"So what do *you* do when no one is around?" She had a playful smirk on her face and didn't realize she was absently petting her belly.

"That is a very personal question, Miss Maggie, and I believe I will plead the Fifth." He stepped toward her and said, "Let's take a look at that cut." Obediently, she held out her hand. He took it in his and brushed his thumb over the thin scab.

"This healed well. That's good."

"Thank you, Doctor Patel."

The phone rang and both Maggie and David jumped and looked in its direction. "Go ahead and get that," said David, as he collected his tools and wiped his hands.

"No, I'm not expecting any calls. It can wait."

The answering machine clicked on and after Maggie's recorded message, Beverly Finker's voice clattered into the room. "Maggie, I stopped by and saw you had a guest. I didn't want to interrupt?" She gave a discreet little cough and went on. "Besides, I'm sure Martin will be home any minute. I wish you would call me back, dear. We need to talk. We seem to be running short on our goals and should stay focused. You *are* the president after—" The answering machine cut her off before she could go on.

David looked at Maggie like she had just been put into the naughty chair in school. "Was that your mother?"

Maggie laughed. "No, it's this overzealous woman, Beverly Finker, who wants to haul everyone who's ever jaywalked into a lineup. I haven't even met her. I don't know how to get rid of her."

The phone rang again and David walked over, picked

up the receiver, and dropped it back into place. "There, chalk up another job well done by David the handyman."

Later, Maggie watched Martin and David talk like they were old acquaintances, and marveled at the detached nature of male conversations. They moved from wiring to sports back to hardware, at which point there was some vacant head nodding on Martin's part, while David discussed voltage requirements. She tried to pay attention to the details of sustaining a superficial conversation and wondered how to hone this skill. There were no strained silences, no awkward pauses. Nor were there any admissions of family deaths or unrequited loves.

Maggie sized up Martin as he stood next to David, the two of them examining the opening where the proposed ceiling fan might go. Both men, while not model handsome, had attractive but different features. If she were playing *Mystery Date* and opened the door to either one, she would have been satisfied. Martin the handsome choirboy and David the artsy, sensitive handyman. There was definitely something about the Mr.-Fix-It/poetry-reading-man fantasy that was as appealing to women as the nurse-angel-of-mercy fantasy was to men.

"Why don't I leave this project unfinished until we can get you guys a ceiling fan you like? I can meet you at

Home Depot some day this week and help you pick one out." David turned to retrieve his tools, which sat on the kitchen counter.

Martin looked at Maggie. "What do you say, Mags?"

Both men turned and looked at her. The innocent request hung in the air like a wind chime, awaiting the gust of an answer to start the music. If she uttered an ill-fitting no based on the heat in her face, the awkward silence would end this pleasant afternoon. If she said yes, then she would commit to another day of confusing attraction-meets-neuroses show-and-tell. David made her feel oddly comfortable and uncomfortable at the same time.

"Sure," she said like it was nothing, like she frequently spent time with semi-strange men who were not her husband. Like she was just a neighbor getting to know another neighbor, and there was nothing between them but a few loose electrical connections.

# *Iceberg*

It was one of those summer nights that people recall when reminiscing about the good old days, all balmy breezes and cicadas. The kind of night that Hollywood pays set technicians thousands of dollars to replicate, hanging the moon, shining the stars. Maggie turned her face toward a gentle gust of air, wheeling her bicycle down the driveway. The baby cartwheeled in her belly.

The houses were dark and tricycles rested quietly on front lawns, worn out after a hard day's play as police cars, motorcycles, and ice cream trucks. She took a deep breath of freedom and exhaled the tightness that often gathered in her sternum. Her mother would call this kind of activity "working the kinks out." Maggie silently agreed. Tyson was a kink all right. A kink in her tidy life of husband, home, and homilies. But after an evening of biking and harassment, she knew she would sleep a dreamless, restful sleep.

Julia stood in her living room, looking out the picture window at her front yard, a chaotic jumble of crab grass, baseball bats, and miniature earth-moving vehicles. She wondered when the Neighborhood Watch would get tired of searching for criminals who probably knew this iceberg was too dull to hit and get after her about her lawn. She could see her ghostlike reflection in the window, superimposed on her neighborhood, a quiet sentinel guarding the block in a short robe.

She slipped her hand into her pocket, felt her fingers brush the soft terrycloth and the tongue-depressor-sized plastic test with the plus sign, indicating pregnancy. She pulled it out and didn't bother looking at it again. The manufacturers had promised an easy read. They were right about that. The inevitability of her condition covered her like a cloak.

Movement to her left caught her eye and she squinted to focus. The night was cloudless and inky, and Julia stepped toward the window and knelt on the couch. Who could possibly be out at this time of night? Someone on a bike? Maybe this Watch thing wasn't such a bad idea. If this was some kid with spray paint, she was a one-woman detention center.

The biker was about to pass under the lamppost in front of Julia's house and she reached for the phone, her finger itching to dial 9-1-1. The streetlight, like the search beam from a lighthouse, caught the figure. It moved from right to left, like Miss Gulch in *The Wizard of Oz.* First the front wheel became illuminated, then the figure's arms, and finally the face. Pajamas, slippers, a white jug of something in her front basket, and an expression of pure bliss. *"Holy shit,"* whispered Julia. Maggie swerved to avoid a puddle from a sun shower earlier in the evening, but caught the edge. Like a child, she lifted her legs off the pedals and held them out to the sides as the bike bumped along, and Julia could almost hear her laughter. *Well,* Julia thought, her disbelief turning to certainty, *it's true, then. The majority of the iceberg* is *buried beneath the surface.*

The weight of the container of bleach on the handlebars created a drag that pulled the bike forward and a little to the left. Maggie shifted her body to the right, and with each pedal stroke she felt strong and purposeful. The shiny penny inside her that was her baby, already familiar with nighttime adventure, kicked with the pleasure of being included. Maggie dropped her hand to her belly and felt the knock. It was one of the reasons she did this middle-of-the-night biking. The baby always woke, and Maggie was reassured by the movement, the life. *We're comrades in arms, you and me. We always will be. You and me against the world*, she thought with considerable calm. Then, as an afterthought, *And daddy, too, of course.*

She coasted to a stop in front of the Tyson house and walked her bike to a large maple tree next to the driveway. Without pause, she grabbed the bleach and rested the jug on her bike seat while she unscrewed the top. She strolled to the center of the lawn and splashed a large portion of the bleach on the grass, hesitated for a moment, as if wondering if the stew she was making needed more salt, then upended the entire contents of the bottle. The smell she associated with white sheets, summer, and clotheslines flew into the air as she spun around on her heel and returned to her bike.

*Against the world.*

## *So Says the Gospel of Julia*

"You look tired. Not sleeping well?" Julia peered closely at Maggie as they rounded a corner and headed up toward the cemetery. It was a day for walking hills, and the sun shone on their heads as they began a gentle climb.

"I look tired?" Maggie asked, not looking at Julia. "Really? I feel pretty good. I sleep like a baby these days. Nothing wakes me up."

"Is that so?" Julia let just a touch of sarcasm slip into the *so*.

"It's this pregnancy; I'm out when my head hits the pillow."

"Not me. My insomnia keeps me up half the night

checking out my tulips. Ironically, I'm the only neighbor who's actually watching." Julia glanced pointedly at Maggie.

"You and Beverly Finker, you mean. As president of the Neighborhood Watch, I thank you." Maggie nodded her head in an official manner. "Still, maybe you should see somebody about that, get some medication. I'd hate to be awake at night."

Julia examined Maggie's appearance but saw nothing atypical: matching jogging suit, hair combed perfectly, nose coat applied. Narrowing her eyes, Julia reached out and gently stopped her friend. "Maggie, do you have something to tell me?"

Breathless after topping a hill, Maggie looked at Julia. "Huh? What do you mean?" There was a mixture of genuine mystification and concern on her face.

"I saw you last night." She paused a minute to let Maggie catch up and then added, "Biking. What the hell were you doing at 3 a.m. pedaling past my house?"

Maggie paused, blinked, and changed tack. "I like it at night. Sometimes I go out and listen to the crickets."

"Oh, come off it. You weren't just outside communing with nature—you were going somewhere. And what's with the jammies and slippers routine?"

"God, simmer down, Julia. What are you, the grand inquisitor? Can't the president of the Neighborhood

Watch go on patrol once in a while?" Maggie was laughing now.

"You are so full of shit. I checked the schedule and that pain-in-the-ass Mrs. Duperman was on last night. You were supposed to be home getting sleep credit for your pregnancy. This is me you're talking to. You might be able to get away with that crap with Martin, or this Beverly person, but I know you. Or I thought I did. You don't just get up in the middle of the night and bike around the neighborhood in your purple pj's without a reason."

They were standing face to face, surrounded by gravestones eternally holding court over the town. Maggie took a deep breath, turned, and said, "Okay, can you just stop yelling at me for a minute?" Then she reached out and touched Julia's forearm, steering her to their favorite gravestone. They sat and Maggie looked directly at Julia. "I go out at night and check on him."

"I assume by 'him' you mean the sex offender."

"Sometimes I leave a . . . a calling card."

"What kind of calling card, Mags?"

"Sometimes I cut the heads off flowers in his yard, or grease his mailbox with Vaseline. I had pizzas delivered to his house once, and last night I dropped a tub of bleach on his lawn. I guess you saw me when I was on my way there."

Julia looked at Maggie, frank surprise on her face, and

then the anger welled inside her like a hot air balloon just before taking flight. "*Stop it,* Maggie," she said too loudly for even a polite nod toward civility. Startled, Maggie looked at Julia with the expression of a puppy who has just been scolded for being a puppy.

"Oh, Jesus Christ, you can't do this. Whatever this is about—Ella, your dad—I don't care, but you've got to stop this obsession."

Maggie reorganized the features of her face in the span of a breath and with an unfamiliar steeliness said, "I'm not asking for your permission."

Momentarily speechless, Julia stared at her friend. A deep worry wrinkle appeared at the bridge of Maggie's nose as if an artist was sketching a new version of her as they sat. Had her jaw always been so set, or was Julia only now noticing? Where had the softness gone in her face? Maggie closed her eyes to the challenge. "I know. I know," Maggie whispered. "I just—"

"You can't keep doing *this*. If I saw you biking around like the Lone Ranger, it's only a matter of time before others do and you *will* get in trouble. Besides, he may call the cops."

"No, I've thought this through. He's not going to call the police. I doubt anyone on the Sex Offender Registry ever wants to contact law enforcement."

"Maybe not, but what if he sees you out there in your

pajamas? Honey, as much as I support your rights for safety, this is dangerous."

Maggie stood abruptly and starting walking out of the cemetery. Her shoulders straightened as she said, "I told you he's only got a secondary sexual assault charge."

"Your trust in the judicial system is second only to your mistrust of men. You watch TV, you know they make deals to lower offenses and reduce sentences. Think about it. I know *I* don't want any kind of sexual delinquent knowing I exist, even one with only a brown belt in offending."

"I'm pretty careful."

"No, you're not. I saw you biking last night with a bottle of bleach in your basket. The only reason I'm willing to have this conversation is because I love you and I'm trying to be your friend."

"Thank you," Maggie said proudly, as if she had been handed a one hundred percent on a spelling test.

"Promise me you will stop this. Enough is enough. I am sure he has gotten the message. Call a meeting. Notify the Watch. Ask for input from the people in that nutty group of yours." Julia clasped her hands together and cracked the knuckles in her right and then left hands. A mannerism from childhood repeated in frustration and full of meaning for Maggie.

"All right, I'll bring it up at the next meeting. I'll try to calm down." Maggie reached for Julia's arm and added, "I just want a normal, safe life."

"Girlie, you passed 'normal' when you decided that biking in your nightie and stalking weirdos was part of your civic duty. But, hey, I'm all for appearing 'normal' if we agree it's just acting. Normal is the kiss of death for an interesting existence. So says the Gospel of Julia."

"Amen," said Maggie wearily.

With the sun in her eyes, Maggie walked away. Her decision was already made. She would have to be more careful. She knew, on some level, that Julia was right. Julia was frequently right—and even when she wasn't, she was mostly supportive. She thought about a memory that lived in her mind like something on a television screen. Her eleventh birthday.

"I hate him," Maggie had cried.

"No, baby, don't say that." Maggie's mother was sitting on the edge of Maggie's bed, stroking her arm. Maggie brushed her mother's hand away.

"I want to say it. I hate him. I hate this stupid life."

"Sweetie."

Snapping her head around to peer at her mother, she said, "How do you know that Daddy's not coming to my birthday dinner? Did you talk to him? What did you say?"

"I didn't talk to him. He was supposed to be here yesterday. I just don't want you to expect him to walk in here. I don't want you to get your hopes up."

"He told me himself he would be here for my birthday. He could still make it. If you were nicer to him maybe he would come home." The second she had uttered the sentence, she had regretted the meanness.

Her mother bent to kiss her and walked out of the room without another word.

It'd been a day of facing facts, all those years ago, the primary fact being that she'd known her father wasn't going to show up even though he had promised. Still, she had known, and stupidly trusted, and worst of all hoped. The day had gone from a rosy, daydreamy A+ birthday to a real world, grayish F– before she had gotten out of bed.

Then Julia arrived.

"Hi, Maggie, happy birthday!" she trilled. "Your mom called my dad and told me to come quick to deliver your breakfast present. Me!" Julia, a sunny puppy hardly able to steady herself, her tail wagging with happiness.

"Are you going to stay and eat with me?" Maggie asked.

"No doubt about it! In fact, I'm staying all day!"

Maggie remembered Julia in her favorite outfit: red skort, purple halter top, and flip-flops. Maggie swiped strawberry on her teeth and for an instant became a zombie. Julia giggled.

"Let's play three wishes," Maggie said.

They'd played this game frequently enough and knew the rules well. You couldn't wish for world peace, like in the Miss America contests, or for a new car for the family or carpeting for the church basement just to get in good with God. It had to be a personal wish. Once you said your wish, no one was allowed to question it.

Without hesitation, Julia said, "I would wish for a bottomless coin purse where the money would keep refilling every time you took some out."

"Oh, that's a good one," Maggie said with admiration. "Would it be a new one or your old George Jetson purse with the Astro zipper pull?"

"I think it would have to be the one I have, otherwise everyone would ask where I got it, and I'd have to explain."

"Yeah, good thinking. What's wish number two?"

"I've been saving this one. Ready? I want to get locked inside Sweets of the World overnight."

Sweets of the World was the candy store in town, where old cedar barrels held every color of saltwater taffy, anise wrapped in red cellophane, and caramel squares. One whole wall was devoted to striped sugar sticks with flavors like cotton candy, watermelon, and lemonade.

On that birthday-wish morning, Maggie did not consider Julia's candy store wish such a good idea. She couldn't imagine finding a cozy place to sleep in Sweets of the World with its sawdust-covered wooden floors and packed-full aisles. Also, having just acquired a bottomless coin purse, you could probably go in and buy whatever you wanted. But rules were rules, so Maggie kept her mouth shut.

Julia's final wish was the one they always finished with: that they would be friends for life, live next door to each other, and marry brothers so they could be at each other's family gatherings.

Julia looked at Maggie eagerly. "Your turn," she said.

"I want to look like Barbara Eden in *I Dream of Jeannie*." Maggie wanted Jeannie's breasts, but she did not have to specify this for Julia; they had discussed it before. She did not want them to grow overnight or anything; that would be freakish.

"I love her genie pants and the inside of her bottle," Julia said with a wistful smile, disappointed she hadn't come up with the idea herself.

"She looks like Barbie, only better. Softer and less tight," said Maggie. There was a quiet moment where each girl imagined herself inside the genie bottle, surrounded by pillows and filmy drapes. With a silky blond ponytail and lovely softball breasts. A beautiful pet girl in a bottle.

Knowing that her third wish was already decided, Maggie carefully considered her second wish. It would, of course, have to do with her father. This was a given. But she also knew she had to be very, very careful. If she wished for her daddy to come home it might be a waste, nothing stopping him from leaving again. She considered wishing that he would return and never leave, but she feared the wish granters might keep him locked forever inside the house. Then he would miss her dance recitals and piano solos. What if Maggie wished for the same daddy, only changed a bit? More reliable. Would he lose some identifiable part of himself? Would she know him when he walked through the door? There was always the possibility that her mother wouldn't be able to identify him, shaven and tidied up.

She sat back against her headboard, exhausted by the monumental task of special ordering the rest of her life. Maggie had looked at Julia and said, "I miss my dad."

Always knowing just what to do, Julia stuffed a strawberry up her nose.

## *A Congregation of Crocodiles*

Julia pushed her way into the drugstore and marched straight back to the condom/pregnancy test/arch support aisle. One-stop shopping.

"Condoms," she said aloud. "Now, there's a thought."

"No, Donald, I told you this morning you need to pick up Thomas after play practice at five o'clock." The emphatic voice of an unknown woman talking on a cell phone pulled Julia's attention away from her goal of purchasing her third pregnancy test. Following the voice, she noticed Maggie's husband, Martin, standing nearby, clearly listening to the conversation.

"Yes, yes, I did. When? When you were brushing your teeth. I think you were on your left incisor." Pause.

"Okay, yes, I'm sorry for being sarcastic. So, please pick up Thomas at the back door of the grade school at five o'clock." A moment passed, and the woman looked at Martin, who was pretending to read a coping-with-the-loss-of-your-pet card. There was a sad tabby on the front with a large tear in her eye. The woman turned her shoulder and lowered her voice, and her exasperation increased.

"You can't? Fine, then. You call the school and tell them that no parent will be picking up Thomas today, so they should just send him off with the nearest child molester." Martin heard the snap of the phone as she broke the connection. And he smiled in recognition of the familiar frustration.

Julia grabbed two boxes promising effective embryo detection under all possible circumstances and strolled to where Martin stood. "Don't you know it's very impolite to eavesdrop?"

Surprised out of his thoughts, Martin turned and saw Julia's familiar smirk.

"How can I help it?" he said with a rueful smile. "Poor Donald."

"What're you doing here?"

"Waiting for a prescription." He replaced the greeting card. "It's actually kind of a relief to know that other men are getting similar treatment from their wives. Of course, these days, I long for Maggie's old micromanagement ways. Lately she's so preoccupied with the Neighborhood Watch that she isn't bothering much with me."

Julia looked sympathetically at Martin, noting his rumpled appearance. "I doubt it. I'm boycotting the whole thing."

"I would be, too, but I'm trying to be supportive." He gave Julia a wistful look. "Maybe I should call that woman's husband, Donald. Have a conversation. He seems nice."

"What would you say to him?"

"Let me think." Martin rolled his eyes to the ceiling. "I'd say, Donald, when did we become children to our wives? Forget to pick up one box of Cheerios from the supermarket and it's nursery school all over again." He shrugged. "I didn't really think it would happen to me. The first time I witnessed the infantilization of a husband was when I saw my brother Paul with his wife. Shelly was so angry at Paul for hanging his jacket on the back of the kitchen chair that she counted to three while waiting for him to pick it up and hang it on the hook with his name on it."

"No way, really?"

"Yeah, what the hell, huh?"

Julia indicated the massive stationery selection in front of them. "You shopping for a card?"

"I dunno. I was looking for one to cheer Maggie up.

No, not cheer her up, exactly. More like return her to earth." He continued as if he were talking to himself. "What is it about women and child molesters? You'd think there was one behind every bush, just lying in wait, casing every corner for an errant father to forget his kid's pickup time and location." He shrugged. "I doubt they have anything for Maggie in this store."

"Just be glad you're not in the market for one of these," Julia said, picking up a sorry-for-your-divorce condolence card. "Can you imagine sending this? Valium, yes, a baseball bat even, but a greeting card?"

"There's one here for everything but what I need. I want one that says 'refocus, please.' Maggie's been so distant and prickly lately. First, she was obsessed with organizing the Neighborhood Watch meeting, and now, I don't know what."

Julia glanced around for an exit and sneaked a peek at her watch.

"For a while she worked feverishly on the baby's room, researching paint for its low fumes and high washability quotient, trying to decide between eggshell or matte finish as if it were key to getting our child into the right college. She brought home paint chip after paint chip and taped them on the wall. She pored over books about furniture placement and read up on the dynamics of feng shui. I don't even know what feng shui is. There were endless monologues about sending the right gender messages with room design, color, even characters from storybooks. I suggested Mickey Mouse and you would have thought I had offered Satan as a roommate for our baby. You know what Maggie said? 'Don't you know that Disney sexualizes every image they produce? Probably even Winnie-the-Pooh has a boner somewhere. There is no way I will ever put an erect Winnie on the walls of my baby's room.' "

As they moved away from the card display, Martin added, "What the hell, I need a card that says, 'I just don't get you' in pointed script."

"Look, Martin, she has some things she has to work out."

He sighed. "When we first met, Maggie was like a *Penthouse Forum* dream girl for a Star Wars geek like me. Pretty, smart, and funny. She was so incredibly sweet and naive, in a way, back then. So sweet to *me*. Plus, you know how she gets things done." He said this with such obvious admiration that Julia felt her throat constrict. "Before quitting her job, she'd saved so much money it kept us solvent for months. But lately I wonder if she might be better off working. All that unchanneled energy is tiring me out. She bounces from one thing to the next. The Neighborhood Watch is just her latest fascination."

*Not really her latest*, thought Julia, but instead she said, "Women go through a tough time during pregnancy,

Martin. Try not to take it too personally. I punched Big Steven in the face during labor. Of course, he had eaten a tuna sandwich just before breathing into my nostrils and telling me to push harder. He totally deserved it."

"Maybe you're right." Martin's gaze dropped to his feet and he said, "On the outside, marriage, babies . . . well, it looks easy. You know, you meet a nice person, you marry her, have a family, go to Disney World on vacation. This is just a lot harder than I thought it would be."

As they talked, they meandered around the store and found themselves in the aisle with kids' music and books. Picking up a *Kid's Rock* CD, Martin read the titles of the songs. " 'Girls Just Want to Make Puns.' What was wrong with the original Cyndi Lauper tune? Was *Fun* un-PC this year?"

"I'm pretty sure Little Steven wouldn't know a pun if it clipped him in the ass. He's still trying to master words with *r*'s in them." Madonna's classic, reimagined as "Like a Sturgeon," was also included on the CD, and Martin decided to buy it. "Maybe this will help me understand children and the world," he said. "I can play it in my car and look for cultural messages."

"Good luck with that. I'm at as much of a loss as you where the world is concerned. Case in point, check out this book. Michael got it for a birthday party." Julia shifted the pregnancy-test kits to her other hand and picked up a book on alligators and crocodiles. She pushed past the pages with photographs of natural habitats and a discussion on evolution. Placing the book in Martin's hands, she pointed to a photo spread of crocodiles of South America. He read the bullet points:

- Crocodiles are cold-blooded and the only animals that hunt humans.
- Female crocodiles will mate for a period of months and seem to enjoy it.
- A female crocodile will defend its nest to the death from any and all animals.
- A congregation of crocodiles will communicate with body language and behavior and are also extremely territorial predators.

"Geez, these seemed like bloodthirsty facts for a kid's book. Do children really need this information?" Martin shook his head. "They take *fun* out of a song on a children's CD but leave the sexual habits of predators in a kid's book. Where's the sense in that? I could go my whole life and not need to know this."

Suddenly Julia touched Martin on the arm and said, "If it makes you feel better, I don't understand what's going on with Maggie, either. But she needs you, Martin. Engaged and paying attention."

Martin scowled defensively. "I am paying attention," he said. "I'm working my ass off so I can take some time when the baby comes."

Julia put her hands up. "Don't shoot the best friend here. I'm just trying to help."

"I know, but how much attention? She gets so mad at me every time I open my mouth."

"That's your job, honey. Lord knows I understand the need for control and unusual entertainment in life. Having had two boys with stereotypical gun-toting, stick-wielding behaviors, I know that a desire for safety *and* a desire for excitement are gigantic opposing forces. It's finding that balance that is probably the true meaning of life. But I don't have the balance, believe me." She shrugged, indicating the pregnancy tests she was carrying. "Just keep an eye on her. I'm not saying any more."

## *Don't Put Your Eggs in One Basket*

"Thanks for coming with me, Mom." Maggie fidgeted next to her mother as they sat in twin floral upholstered chairs in the doctor's waiting room. "They're usually good about staying on time for appointments. They like to keep us unpredictable, hormone-filled balloons on schedule." She laughed weakly and smoothed her bangs.

"I'm glad you called. Just relax. Everything is fine." Her mother patted her leg and pulled out a paperback novel. Maggie glanced around for some reading material. A *Scientific American* sat shading itself with superiority underneath a rubber plant.

She nudged her mother and indicated the magazine. "I already feel like my own biosphere. I don't want to read a serious science article. How about some Hollywood gossip or maybe a *Psychology Today*? That one might be helpful." She laughed again and noticed a *Better Homes and Gardens* being stripped of an article about a ten-day diet by a woman who, in Maggie's opinion, would need more than ten days. She bounced her legs and looked around.

Maggie finally settled on the *Scientific American* and began rapidly flipping pages while scanning the waiting room. Four other pregnant women sat serenely, reading, chatting on their cell phones, or gazing into space. Maggie took a deep breath and exhaled. She glanced at the open magazine in her lap and a full-page photo of a naked brain caught her attention. On the opposite page, Maggie read a bolded sentence centered within an otherwise bland text.

"Mom, listen to this, 'Evidence supports the notion that the amygdala is responsible for generating fear, while the basal ganglia appears to be the seat of positive emotion—namely happiness.' "

"Huh," her mother said, without interest.

Maggie turned toward her mother for emphasis as she spoke. "*Better Homes* is publishing another 'Best Chocolate Cake Ever' while right here in this *Scientific American*, they are defining and explaining my own personal brain structure." A little too loudly, she added, "I bet they have a diagram."

The mannish woman at the check-in counter glanced up quickly. Maggie crossed her leg and jiggled her foot while searching the pages of the magazine. "If it were *my* cranium, there would be a huge, bulbous fearful amygdala sitting next to a petite, overpolite if not happy basal ganglia. 'Don't mind me,' my cheerful ganglia would say. 'I'm happy shoveling the serotonin.'" A new mother with an infant in an Easter basket–like car seat picked up her child and moved. Maggie's mother sat up in mild alarm, watching her daughter adopt the guilty posture and technique of the weight-conscious *Better Homes* reader. Maggie coughed and tore out the article and subscription card and stuffed it into her purse.

"What in the world are you doing?"

"I'm fine, Mom. While women in the rest of the world are redecorating their foyers, I'm going to spend my spare time brain mapping. I'm going to visualize stronger, more victorious basal ganglia." She stood up abruptly, dropping the magazine to the floor. "I can't go in there. I'm *not* going in there." Without waiting for a response, she turned and headed out the electric double doors, which parted with practiced cooperation.

Maggie rushed to her van with her mother on her heels.

"Wait! Where are you going?"

Unlocking and pulling the door open, Maggie sat and

started the car, all in one fluid movement. Her mother was able to get the passenger-side door open fast enough to say, "Wait!" She pulled herself into the van, breathing hard, and looked at her daughter. "Where are you going? What's going on with you?"

Maggie sat panting, her eyes darting around. Gripping the steering wheel, she said, "Shut the door, Mom."

"No, I won't. Honey, take a deep breath and calm down."

"Please. Just shut the door."

"That's quite enough, Maggie Elizabeth. You are not going to unravel right here in the parking lot of Doctor Ng's office." She reached for the key and snapped the engine off.

As the sound of the motor died, Maggie said, "Don't put your eggs in one basket."

"What?" Her mother reached for Maggie's purse. "Give me your phone. I'm going to call Martin."

"No, don't." Maggie put her head between her fingertips on the steering wheel and breathed, "God, it's hot in here." She opened her door and pulled at the neck of her T-shirt. "I know we don't talk about stuff. I mean, I never told you. I guess I didn't tell anyone, really." Maggie rested her head back onto her steering wheel. "After Ella died, greeting card phrases popped into my brain nonstop. You know, 'a picture paints a thousand words.' 'Every stick has two ends.' 'Cold hands, warm heart.' Like this weird chipper part of my head was rooting around for an expression that would help me find meaning in such a tragedy and cheer me up. It was as if my mind was so used to problem solving it couldn't sit idly by without trying to help." Maggie swallowed hard. "'Every cloud has a silver lining.' 'Silence is golden.' I was holding the healthiest-looking, lifeless child there ever was." Maggie paused, not wanting to leave this moment in her narrative—a moment she often revisited just to feel the weight and depth of her child once again. "The phrase that haunts me, the cautionary synapse that fires again and again in warning is: 'Don't put all your eggs in one basket.' It wakes me up at night, Mom. I can't sleep because of it."

"Oh, Maggie, don't do this." She touched her daughter's arm, warm but covered in goose bumps.

"I remember the doctor trying to explain what happened, and I just wanted to curl into a mother-child burrito and tell the world to rot away. Instead, I had to form words into full sentences. Make funeral plans." She rooted around in her purse and pulled out a blue water bottle with the words "Tabor Clinics: Health Care for People" on it. "Martin, I'm sorry to say, was worthless. He was like a coach for the big conference championship. Just before the doctor came in, he said, 'Okay, Mags, put your game face on.' I wanted to shove him into the next state, but I would have dropped . . . her. I did manage to knock him good once and it felt great . . . at the time." She took a long sip of water and then another. "The hardest part of that terrible day, by far, was handing Ella to the nurses for *aftercare*. I remember thinking that this was the most ridiculous of systems. I should have been able to hold her next to me until she dissolved into my pores like nourishing facial cream. I can't do that again."

"Oh, baby, you won't have to."

"Remember at Ella's funeral? All those well-meaning friends preaching, 'God only doles out what you can manage.' You know what I think? I think God doles out exactly what you can't handle and the test is to exceed his expectations. And you know what? That just sucks."

Maggie's mother pushed the van's armrests up and out of the way. She inched her body closer to her daughter's and awkwardly held her. "This time, everything is going to be just fine," she said. "You'll see."

"Martin is always telling me to relax, but details and tasks are what keep me going. Without this glue, it's a short trip off the curb into the gutter, and anyone who doesn't believe that never lost a child." She paused for a moment and added, "This is what you learn after the death of a child. The consolation prize. Consolation wisdom."

Her mother helped her to an upright position and took her daughter's face between her hands. She wiped sweat and tears with her fingers and said, "How could you *not* put all your eggs in one basket? This is precisely what happens, *what must happen*, when a woman gets pregnant and agrees to have a child. Whether you know it or not, you take your sanity, fold it, and tuck it into your children's hearts, and they carry it with them unceremoniously and unaware." She patted her daughter's sternum. "You have always held mine, right here. And this one"—she indicated Maggie's belly—"will always hold yours. That, my darling girl, is both the hard and soft candy center of life. You just can't get one without the other. It's a twofer every time. Besides, you not only *can* do it, but you *have* to do it."

Maggie pushed back. Inhaling deeply, she exhaled and placed her hands on the mound of her belly, the globe that would become her entire world. "I can do this." She shot a quick glance at her mother. "Not today, mind you. I'm not going back in that doctor's office today, so don't say another word about it." Closing her eyes, she stretched her legs and pictured her basal ganglia wrestling her amygdala to the ground. "Say uncle," she said.

## *Cold Crankin' Amps*

Sitting in the sun, on the back steps of her house, Maggie drummed her fingers and consulted her spreadsheet for documenting Tyson's movements. So much open space, so many blank timeslots. Julia had derailed Maggie's surveillance duties with her discovery, which forced Maggie to understand two things. She had to be less visible, and she had to get to work. The next Neighborhood Watch meeting was only three weeks away.

Maggie wrote with her pencil *Continue surveillance duties* in several places on her weekly list and *Make doctor's appointment* as if they were insignificant details of an ordinary life. *Buy apples, Fold laundry, Fight crime, Make sure the baby is okay.* She shook her head and sharpened her pencil.

She pulled her daily list forward and drew a sharp line under *David* and *Ceiling fan*, breaking the point off her pencil and poking a punctuation mark right through the paper. The telephone rang.

"Hello?"

"Hi, hon. Is David there yet?"

Maggie released a breath through her bangs. "Martin," she said. With measured patience, she added, "No, not yet. I thought you might be him."

"Okay. Well, when he gets there, could you ask him to look at the latch on the back door?"

"I fixed that." Standing, she walked into the house.

"You did? When?"

Maggie looked at her fingers. The skin around her thumbnails was pink and fresh. She hid them from sight. "I don't know, Martin, a while ago. That is the least of my worries right now. Seriously. The very least."

A silent slice of time sat between them and the phone beeped. "I've got another call, Mags. I've got to get this. You okay then? Everything good?"

Maggie rolled her eyes to an invisible audience and said with sarcasm, "Fabulous, honey."

"See you tonight, then."

Maggie replaced the phone. Good old Martin. He was oblivious to anything that wasn't easily identified with clues and cartoon balloons. She often thought that if she ran through the house with an airplane banner behind her, it would help their communication. *Attracted to maintenance man, stalking a predator, dinner's in the oven!*

It was Martin's expectation of a kind of generic, disinfected, normalcy that was irritating. He was no fuss, so he wanted no fuss. As if people could choose it from a menu of options from God. "Yes, I'll take the life without fracas please. Two of these with a side salad should do it. Dressing on the side."

Maggie checked her reflection in the window, smoothed her hair, and straightened her new maternity top. She punched the button on her radio and, in spite of herself, began tapping her running shoe. Grabbing her coffee cup she moved her head to the rhythm of a country song. At the coffeemaker she inched her shoulders, put down her cup, and tried a little turn, knocking a chair to the floor with her hip. The ringing of the phone interrupted her and she closed her eyes in irritation.

"What d'ya need, Martin?"

"Maggie? This is David. I've been at your front door, knocking, but I wasn't sure you could hear me above the music."

"David!" Maggie silenced the radio with a snap and said, "God, sorry, I'll come get you." Rushing to the door, she undid the lock and wrenched the door open. Speaking to David both in person and on the phone she was holding, she said, "I was listening to music." Then, with a nod, "Obviously."

David, still speaking into his phone, said, "Having your own rock star moment?"

"Absolutely," she said, at last putting her phone away. With her chin up in a challenge, she added, "Pregnant gals can rock, you know."

"I'm certain they can. It's just that you don't see many of them on stage."

"That's just typical American oppression for you. Keep those moms home cookin' instead of rockin'." Laughing, she turned away from the door and walked down the hall toward the kitchen. "I always wanted to be in a band," she confessed. "It almost happened when I was in college. We were going to be called Cold Crankin' Amps. You know, like on a car battery."

David followed her into the kitchen. "Good name. So what happened?"

"Oh, we really just had the name. No one could sing and I was the only one who could play an instrument."

"Yeah? Which one?"

"Clarinet."

"Not much call for clarinet in rock 'n' roll."

"No, not much call," she admitted.

Their conversation sputtered and rolled to a stop. The coffeemaker gurgled, and Maggie tugged her earlobe and sighed. She looked at David and with a single shoulder shrug said, "Life, huh? It's always so hard. Apparently you need more than a name to start a band. And just because you know some words, it doesn't always mean you can carry a conversation." And to herself she thought, *And a nighttime ride on a bike cannot entirely change who you are.*

David matched her shrug with one of his own. "What d'ya say we go pick out a fan."

"Let's do it. I'll drive," she said and grabbed her car keys from the hook by the door.

"You're not one of those men too cool to ride in a minivan, are you?"

"Not if you're chauffeuring," David said and winked.

Maggie replied, "Are you saying you trust me to get you there safely, then?"

"Absolutely, and with style." David wore a green T-shirt with the words *Eat Your Vegetables* printed on it and a pair of khakis with frayed pockets and cuffs. He reminded Maggie of a commercial for casual living, the kind where you admire the nonchalant confidence of the model while he does ordinary tasks like packing the van or throwing a football.

"Get in. But if you slam down an imaginary brake at every intersection, you can drive yourself."

"I promise I will not be putting on any brakes today." Maggie flashed a look at his expression for clarification, but his head was turned while he pulled the passenger door shut. She fidgeted in the silence and wondered if he could sense her frenetic brain activity rooting around for a topic of conversation. Turning left onto the highway, she pulled the overhead visor down and squinted into the sun.

"Look at that sun coming through the clouds like the heavenly host," she said. "Can you believe that some people don't believe in God?" He looked at her with raised eyebrows and she continued.

"I don't care what the scientists say about particulate matter and contrails. If the combination of dust and airplane exhaust comes out looking this beautiful, it has to have been designed by some higher power."

"You've got a point. He makes a lot of beautiful things."

Sliding a sideways glance over to him, she said, "Don't get ahead of yourself, cowboy. Who said God was a *he*?"

"I've just always assumed God was a man. Look at the job he did on women, making them pleasing to the eye. He sure didn't take as much time with men."

"You apparently haven't seen the Reynolds boy mowing the lawn." Maggie let out a low whistle. She felt thrilled by her daring. David laughed and Maggie looked at his face. When he laughed, it was the reward of summer. Maggie found herself working hard for sunshine.

"That's what you do all day, gaze at lawn boys and rock out?"

"Everyone needs a hobby."

"I can't argue with you there."

Suddenly, it was a glorious afternoon. She was driving with a man who was not her husband, making conversation like a pro, and her pores were tiny and amazing. Yes, she was married and pregnant, but this made everything feel safe, distanced.

"Actually," Maggie said, "if we're talking deity gender, God has to be a woman. Do you think a man would have the foresight to create a fully functioning universe complete with the check and balance of evolution? Martin can't anticipate when we might need more milk, let alone an ark with two of every animal. And he's one of the smarter ones of your species—no offense."

"None taken, but don't you think that argues for man as creator? He made the ultimate helpmate so he could just sit back and take in the scenery."

"Yes, and that is exactly what is happening today," she said with a sly smile. "You're going to put in a ceiling fan while I sip my coffee."

"Hmmm. You win," David said, grinning, and he looked out the window with his smile.

After exhaustively discussing the merits of each ceiling fan available—engine, price, and appearance—they chose one and checked out of the huge home-warehouse retail store. David loaded the box into the car. As Maggie watched him walk in front of her, she wondered if people thought they were a couple. A married pair running errands before the baby comes, laughing and talking about what to have for dinner. She was so immersed in her fantasy television commercial that when they were back on the road and discussing lunch options, she nearly called him "Honey."

They drove to a deli and bought one fat roast beef sandwich, a pickle, and a container of fruit cocktail to share. They ate at the fountain in the center of town, watching the noontime walkers, the toddlers dipping their fingers into the cool water, and their tired mothers, who had come hoping to have an adult conversation before heading home for naptime.

"This is the fountain Beverly Finker wants to put a camera on," Maggie pointed out.

"Because of the soap vandals?"

"Right you are. The Slippery Soap Scandal of Elmwood, Wisconsin."

"How is Mrs. Finker these days?" David asked.

"She hasn't called since you hung up on her the other day. Thank you again for that."

"It won't be your last encounter."

Maggie stopped chewing and spoke around her bite of pickle. "Do you know her?"

"You could say that. She's had her witch hunts going for years. I remember her when I was in high school. She's a meddlesome hag."

Maggie scrutinized David's face, waited for a softening and found none. "At first I thought she might be some help with the Neighborhood Watch," she said, "but now I'm thinking we are not of the same mind."

David cleared his throat, shedding his impassive look, and said, "What, exactly, are you trying to accomplish with the Neighborhood Watch?"

"To be honest, I don't know. Martin and Julia want me to give it up. They just don't understand."

"What do they need to understand?"

"Before my dad died, he used to drink and disappear . . . a lot. I think because I never had any say in whether he was home or not, every moment of my childhood was two-thirds full of questions, all about my parents." She pushed her bangs up away from her face, shrugged, and went on. "So only one-third of my thoughts were ever left for me. It kept me preoccupied all the time. So, I haven't always seen trouble before it crashes into me."

"How does the Neighborhood Watch help you with that?" David's eyes were calm and interested. He had stopped eating and was fully focused on their conversation.

"I thought if I organized something of my own . . . you know, a kind of lookout, a preemptive strike against potential danger . . . Maybe I would be less blindsided, more in control."

"I'm not going to say I don't know how you feel. Life is like Russian roulette. And you never know who has the loaded gun." He sat without speaking, took a sip of milk, and continued. "Still, I think *you* should be able to define you, and not let others do the job. No matter who else had their hands in things."

Maggie tilted her head and said, "Yes, that's what I'm trying to do. Decide. Do. Take control."

David leaned back and fiddled with the plastic wrap from his sandwich. "Control is more slippery than the soap in this fountain. Just when you think you have it, it will fly out of your hands without fanfare."

Maggie considered this as they shared their sandwich. "You came to the meeting. You must think it's a good idea."

David said, not unkindly, "It's an idea, that's for sure. But I really came to see what people were afraid of. Who was in charge. What plans were brewing."

"I see. Writer as observer."

"I guess. I do like to keep my eyes open."

She watched a sesame seed rest in the corner of his mouth until his tongue flicked out and pulled it inside. Maggie wiped her fingers and said, "There are days when I can leave control behind. You know, days like today."

She began to try to clarify, stopped, and started collecting their garbage instead. She stuffed the salad container with the forks and wrappings and then said, "Do you mind if we take a detour? Baby Bountiful called and our crib came in. Plus, I need a pair of jeans."

"I'm all yours today. Do with me what you will."

At Baby Bountiful, David helped the store clerk load the crib into the van while Maggie pulled jeans off the racks to try on. She wrinkled her nose at her clothing reality—elastic panels, no pockets, and cotton/polyester fabric. She pulled on the first pair. Peeking out from the curtain, she saw David sitting quietly in a pink overstuffed armchair eyeing a mannequin with a large belly and protruding nipples. Embarrassed for David, herself, and especially for the immodest six-foot-tall plastic dummy, she called, "I'll be right out."

"No rush. Take your time," he said, and Maggie glanced out again, pretending that he was her husband and she was his pregnant wife. He looked up and caught her gaze and smiled his crinkled grin.

As they left the store, Maggie looked past her vehicle. At the end of the street, she saw a gray van with its blinker on, turning left away from town. Startled, she grabbed David's arm. "Do you see that van?" Her voice went up a notch. "There, at the end of the block. It's turning."

David looked up. "Yes?"

Excited, Maggie said, "I've seen it before. Lots of times. Do you know who owns it?"

"No idea. Why? Is that important?"

Slightly out of breath, she glanced at David. She was standing very close to him, so close that her belly brushed his forearm. She let go of his arm and said, "I just . . ." She took a breath. "It just seems like I see it everywhere when I'm out."

"Well, it's a small town," David pointed out. "Have you seen it do something wrong?" He opened Maggie's door and placed his hand in the small of her back. His hand was warm.

"No. Maybe. I think the whole crime-watch thing is getting to me. I should give it up."

"Everybody needs a hobby," he said without a smile.

When they returned to her house, David got to work on the ceiling fan while Maggie attempted the crib assembly.

"David," she called into the kitchen. "Can you come in and hold something for me?"

David took the side of the crib and held it as Maggie balanced the metal supports and screwed them into place. "You're pretty good with a screwdriver, little lady."

"Like I said the other night, my instrument of choice is the butter knife, but if I have to use a real tool, I can make do."

"How's your energy? Are you tired? My mom says that being pregnant is like wearing a magical sleep robe every hour of the day."

"Actually," Maggie said, "I feel both awake and alert right now. Sort of like the way I get after a whole can of soda, the crack cocaine of the sleepy but health conscious.

He grinned and said, "Do you read much?"

She stopped working and held the screwdriver as she spoke. "I try to," she said, "but at night this baby is like a huge, abdominal sleeping pill. I only get through the first paragraph of any given book over and over again until I have to return it to the library. What about you, what are you reading now?"

"Lately I've been reading a lot of comic books, especially the ones about superheroes with shields. It's the regular guy that turns me on, the one with no special powers, doing right for America," he said. "I like the idea of any Joe Schmo working for the greater good. You know, the hero within."

"So, what superhero are you, Fix-It Man? Ventilating stagnant kitchens one ceiling fan at a time?"

"More like Lame-Man. Impressing pregnant women with skills learned in middle school."

"Hey, don't shortchange yourself or your talent. Women like a guy who can turn a screw." She froze, realizing her word choice. She would have liked to poke Freud in the eye, he with his unconscious slips and sexual innuendo.

But David didn't acknowledge her gaffe. "My grandfather tinkered around all day. If I wanted to spend time with him, it required a working language of voltage and tubing. I think he believed all life's philosophies could be explained by repairing a dimmer switch or rewiring a bathroom."

"Wise man." Maggie hesitated. "By the way, thanks for ignoring my previous comment. I don't get out with people much."

"You owe me."

She looked at his hands while he worked. She had to stop herself from reaching out to touch a black blood blister in the middle of his left thumbnail.

David stood up from the floor where they had been working on the crib, arched his back to stretch, and said, "It's late, I'd better go." At that moment Maggie and David pushed to the surface of the day and popped through into reality. "My mom is making meatloaf. I'm not sure how many more dinners I'll be having at home, so I hate to miss real food."

Maggie looked up with a question in her eyes. "Why?" she asked. "Are you thinking of taking an evening job?"

"No. I move around a lot, and I think my mom can handle life without me soon. I like to write from different locations; it keeps my perspective fresh."

"How do you know when you need a new venue?" she asked, getting up and following him to the door. There was a tiny pull in her chest and she slowed to put some distance between them.

"It's written in the wind," he said with a wink. Maggie waved as he got into his car and drove down her driveway. He beeped once and stuck his hand out, holding a peace sign in the air. She watched from the front step until he dropped his hand to the car door and patted out a rhythm on the metal.

Later that evening, Maggie called Julia to help her translate the day into something understandable and to make sure the air between them was breathable. There was a loud clatter of noise in the background as Julia spoke through the phone.

"What has gotten into you lately?" Julia's attitude was as clear as if she was standing with Maggie in her living room, shaking her finger. "I can't believe you spent the day lolling around and chatting with a single man. Aren't you supposed to be hard at work researching New Math for the bambino and reading up on epidurals?" Julia's voice became muffled as she covered the phone receiver with her hand and lobbed a caution at her son. "Little Steven, if you hit Mikey with that ball, it's the timeout chair for you."

Maggie spoke through the rumpus. "I thought you'd be happy to know that I'm branching out, trusting people, obsessing less about sex offenders. Besides, we weren't lolling, we were getting things done while socializing."

Julia sneered at her son. "Michael, if you ask me anything while I'm on the phone, the answer is no." Then to Maggie, she said, "Sorry, it's a zoo here. Who are you kidding, Maggie? Socializing for you is attending a cookware party and buying a whisk, not hanging around the hardware store with some cute guy. You'd better be careful, or the Neighborhood Watch is going to put a scarlet 'A' on your mailbox."

"Don't be ridiculous. He's engaged. Probably a bit bored, too, since his fiancée is abroad. We're a good pair; I'm engorged and a lot bored, too."

Not even bothering to cover the mouthpiece this time, Julia shouted, "I'm going into the closet, boys, and when I come out you had better have picked up your crap." The background noises became subdued and she continued, "Okay then, sweetie, I'll bite. Tell me about this David, something other than that he knows where your fuse box is."

"You couldn't stop yourself, could you?"

"Absolutely not." Julia laughed. Then there was a loud bang and she yelled, "No, you cannot come in here." In a quieter voice she said, "So help me, if Big Steven doesn't come home and take these little monsters to the park, I'm going to be arrested for shaken-husband syndrome."

"You want me to call you back?"

"You think it would be any different later? It's *always* chaos. What do you like about this David guy?"

Maggie thought a minute. "It's like he's a stir stick in my black-coffee personality. Usually, I'm just plain old coffee, but when David is around I become a Frappuccino. It's like somehow I get to try out a fearless, funny, flirtatious personality."

"Flirtatious, huh?" Julia paused. Then with less than her usual verve said, "I know you don't need to hear this from me, but you be careful, Maggie. He's a real person, a grown man, not just a pet boy you get to try out your new flirty-girl personality on."

Maggie sighed, acknowledging with her exhale that Julia had made a good point. She lifted her eyes to the ceiling. "But I repeat: He's engaged; I'm married and great with child. It's the safest scenario to try out a new personality; maybe I'll keep it."

"Shit," Julia said, abruptly changing the subject. "It's too quiet out there; I gotta hang up and get out of this closet. But have you asked Martin whether he thinks you need a new personality? Maybe he likes the old one. Maybe we all do."

## *Prenatal Meticulitis*

Maggie hefted herself up, her legs restless and twitchy. She longed to be able to lie on her belly without picturing her flattened child, pug-faced and irritated, elbowing for space. It had stopped raining and she needed to get outside to the impossibly perfect moon. She inhaled and let her mind follow its practiced path to the memory of Ella's lips, her paper-thin eyelids, the tiny blue vein in her wrist. She stroked Ella's face with her breathy thoughts and the fragile memory faded.

Before Ella, Maggie's maternal feelings had been on par with those of Joan Crawford or that mother in *Lolita*: cigarette, hand on hip, too much lipstick. She had worried that if her nurturing biology didn't step up to the plate, she would never forgive her child for labor and delivery, let alone stretch marks. Now she knew the naiveté of such a concern. She would forgive her child of anything—poor grades, career confusion, mass murder.

Maggie pushed herself up to a sitting position. Looked at the clock. Midnight. "Where the hell is Martin?" she wondered out loud.

Swinging her legs out of bed, she stuffed her bare feet into her already tied running shoes. She scuffed her way to the closet and removed an old yellow rain slicker with a pattern of green frogs lining the hood. Grabbing a baseball hat, she moved quickly downstairs. Urgent to get out of the house, Maggie searched for her keys, ransacking a quilted backpack she had recently begun using as a purse. When she heard Martin arriving home, she jerked her head up and stopped moving, tucking herself into the shadows of the kitchen.

Maggie watched as Martin fumbled with the door handle and strode into the house. He tossed his house keys into the air and caught them with one hand, pumping that hand in the air with flourish. He hummed a toneless tune, finishing with a little quiet countertop percussion. Stopping, he listened, swaying slightly. The house was silent, the kitchen spotless down to the white folded kitchen towels hanging from the oven handle. He shook his head with appreciation and flipped on the overhead light. When the usual sputter and pull of electricity was replaced with a quiet whirring and a light breeze, Martin looked up to find a large ceiling fan in place of the old globe fixture he was used to seeing.

Maggie stepped forward as Martin's eyes became accustomed to the light. "Hey," she said.

He jumped. "What the hell! Maggie, wh–what are you doing up?"

"Waiting for you. It's late. Where have you been?"

"It's softball night, remember?" Examining her troubled face and mistaking her expression for concern, he said, "Aw, honey, did you forget?" He stepped closer and awkwardly planted a poorly aimed kiss on her left eyelid.

She ducked away from him and said, "You've been drinking."

"Yeah, but jus' a couple. With the guys."

Maggie rolled her eyes. "The guys." She made a disgusted noise in the back of her throat. "You've been gone for hours."

He made a play at examining his watch, squinted, and gave up. "Well, yeah. But it's softball night." He looked at Maggie with an imploring expression that changed when he noticed her coat. "Why're you wearing that? Were you coming to look for me?"

Maggie's eyes darted to her keys hanging on the peg at the back door and then back to her husband. Avoiding the question, she said, "I wouldn't know where to begin to look." She narrowed her eyes. "You're loaded."

"I deserve it! I caught a fly ball and made two hits that contributed to runs." He slipped on the middle syllables of *contributed*, mimicking the running of the bases, the slide into home plate. The next sentence came out clearly, as if he were a thespian. "I sealed the team's win and a place in the tournament." He put his hands in the air like he was running through a finish line. Then cupping his fingers over his mouth and exhaling, he made the "crowd goes wild" sound.

Martin dropped his head, laughing quietly. Slipping off one of his cleats, he shuffled to the fridge, one shoe on, the other off. He blinked in the refrigerator light. "No dinner, huh?"

"I . . . I didn't make dinner." Maggie glanced down at her ridiculous getup and smoothed her pajamas over her belly.

"Bread, mustard, ketchup, eggs. This is some victory dinner: condiments and eggs on toast." He grabbed the milk, shut the refrigerator door, and rummaged for some cereal from the cabinet near the stove. "The gladiator arrives back from battle and is met at the door with a high-fiber cereal. This is truly dinner porn." He dropped the spoon and he bent to pick it up, taking a step back to steady himself.

"You could have called. I've just been sitting here." She spoke in the quiet, good-girl voice she learned from her mother as a child.

He stared at his food. His good mood sputtered as the sound of a motorcycle accelerated, changed gears, and screeched out of range. He started to hum again but his voice bumped into the quiet, and the hen and rooster salt-shakers on the stovetop looked annoyed and seemed to shush him.

"I wish you had been there, Mags."

"Well, then you should have invited me, Martin."

"You wouldn't have come."

"That's because I can't hang around with a bunch of has-been athletes reliving their old prowess. Memoirs of an athlete, a verbal history handed down in barrooms across the country. I like that you suck at sports. I thought you'd be home more. You used to be home more."

Glancing at the pile of recyclables, Martin noticed the flattened crib box. He recognized the smiling couple holding a chubby baby gazing lovingly at the crib. "I thought we were going to set the crib up together?"

"My point exactly. You'd have to be home for that."

Pulling the baseball cap off, he ran his hand through his hair. "Aw, don't be mad. This night has been by far the best night of athletics in my life."

"I need you, Martin. Not running out the door to

work, not bragging about some stupid softball pitch, and certainly not drunk."

His head down, he spoke into his cereal bowl, "You don't."

"What?" Maggie was now staring pointedly at her husband.

"You don't need me. You're like a dog on his own walk. You have prenatal meticulitis and you're a one-woman show."

Stepping back like she had received a blow, she said, "It's a damn good thing I'm self-sufficient because you, my friend, are no help. I don't see you setting up the crib or buying diapers." She spun on her heel and grabbed her car keys. "I need some air."

Maggie pushed out the door before Martin could protest. He gazed at his shoeless foot, his big toe poking through a large frayed hole.

"Maggie! Don't! Where are you going?" Stopping short of the door, he threw his hands out in front of him, a gesture he'd often seen his father use that said he was finished. His hands washed in futility. He reached down and yanked the other cleat off his foot, throwing it at the back door.

"Fuck it. Just fuck it!"

Turning, he shuffled into the living room and dropped into his man-chair, as Maggie liked to call it. Black leather with a pocket for the remote. A recliner where, she said, testosterone is king. Maggie wouldn't go near it, saying if she fell asleep in it while watching *When Harry Met Sally*, she would wake up to *Die Hard* having sprouted a goatee. He could hear her back the car out of the garage.

His head spun a little and he was suddenly very tired. He pushed the Power button and the television brightened to an infomercial extolling the virtues of healthy AAAs: arms, abdominals, and assets. The announcer was a tight, fibrous man with skin that looked like the covering on a baked ham. Martin was sure there was a clip somewhere in the top of the man's head that, when released, would shed his skin like an old man's pants. He was speaking effortlessly to the camera, straddling a woman who was sliding up and down on an elevated board. Apparently he was spotting her in some way, while she slid to crotch level. She paused momentarily, and with a teasing smile at the audience, pulled herself to a more hygienic, PG-rated position.

The couple on the television wore black, extremely tight exercise clothes, and Martin looked at his own sportswear—a pair of gray sweatpants with a ripped seam at the crotch and an old Ohio State sweatshirt. He rolled up his shirt and looked at his belly. He wasn't fat, but he wasn't muscular either. His abs were tight but it was probably more abdominal wall than six-pack, love-machine muscle. He held his breath to flex, gave up, and exhaled grimly. He considered the couple on the screen—tan, oiled, in-synch, sexy. Scratch that, really sexy.

Concentrating on the number on the screen, he reached for the telephone. Listening for the dial tone, he waited. He replaced the phone and listened again. It sounded as if someone was on the line.

"Hello? Is someone there?"

There was a momentary pause and a woman's voice came on. "Yes, is this Mr. Finley?"

"Can I help you?"

"This is Beverly Finker calling."

"I'm sorry, Mrs. Finker. Maggie can't come to the phone."

"Oh yes, of course not. Well, then could you give her a message for me? Please tell her that I'd be happy to take her patrolling schedule. I just don't think it's safe for her to be out biking at night in her condition. She could fall or get into an accident of some sort."

"Biking? No, I'm sure you're right. Thanks, Mrs. Finker."

"No worries, as the kids say. Have her call me if she'd like. I've been waiting."

Martin hung up the phone with a puzzled expression on his face and said out loud, "As the kids say, bat-shit crazy fer sher." Getting out of his chair, he moved stiffly to the floor. Looking at the ceiling, he put his hands behind his head, rolled onto his side, and fell immediately asleep.

Maggie slammed the van in reverse and sped out of the driveway. Jamming the transmission into Drive, she stopped and took a breath. She hit the electric buttons on her armrest to open all the windows, feeling the damp night air on her face. Then she made a decision and gunned the accelerator. As she approached Tyson's house, she leaned on the horn and blasted it down the entire block. The clear, screaming horn broke through the peace of the summer night. She slowed, grabbed the armrest, and turned the corner too fast. Hitting the Dickenson's driveway, she plowed ten feet through their golf course of a lawn, then bumped over the curb and back into the street. Maggie supported her belly, revved the engine, and headed for downtown. Her thoughts darting and distracting, she sped through the buttoned-up village. Tuesday night in Elmwood. *Woo-hoo.*

The flashing red and blue lights confused her when she looked into the rearview mirror. Her right leg reflexively hit the accelerator, and the car shot forward with a jolt. Shocked, she moved her foot to the brake and brought the car to a herky-jerky stop.

"Shit." She closed her eyes. "God, no." Maggie squeezed her hands into fists and pressed them to her eyes. After rolling the window down, she rummaged for her purse. "I know I was speeding," she said when the officer approached. "I'm sorry." She could feel the pulse in her throat, right in the middle of her chagrin.

The police officer stood with a large tubular flashlight at his hip. He shined the light into Maggie's face and around the seats of her van. "Where're you going in such a hurry at this time of night?"

She hesitated, then sputtered, "My mother's condo. She called me; she isn't well. She gets scared all alone."

The policeman lifted Maggie's license from her hand and shined his light onto the laminated square. He studied her face for a long moment.

"Maggie Finley. Why is that name familiar?"

Confused, Maggie said, "I don't know." Squinting at the officer's face, she tried to remember if she'd ever seen him before.

As the man concentrated on her license, she noticed he was older than she originally thought, not much younger than her mother.

"I know now," he said. "Aren't you the woman who called to have a law enforcement representative at a Neighborhood Watch meeting? Finley. Yeah. Something about how to recognize suspicious behavior?"

Relieved, Maggie sighed, "Yes, that was me. I'm the president of the Watch."

He folded his lower lip into his mustache and said, "I'd hate to give the president of a concerned citizens group a ticket for speeding, Mrs. Finley. That's not very good role-modeling on your part. We're supposed to be on the same side."

Maggie dropped her head and twirled her wedding band.

He cleared his throat, handed back her license and said, "I'm going to let you go with a warning. Please drive safely and slowly to your mother's."

Maggie swallowed hard and nodded. She felt the prickling behind her nose. Her eyes wet, she tried to look again at the officer, to thank him, but he had turned after gently bumping his closed fist off the roof of her car. "Take it easy, ma'am. Let's make sure the next time I see you it will be at that meeting."

Maggie hauled open the heavy security door of her mother's condo and trudged down the hall. Bleary-faced and wild-haired, she watched her mother step out of her apartment

"What in the world?" Maggie's mother reached for her daughter, with concern etched in every crease and crinkle.

She took her daughter's arm and reached to support her belly, which pushed through the silly rain slicker. "C'mon inside. What's going on?"

"Oh, Mom. I made a huge mistake."

Pushing the hair off Maggie's face, she tilted her daughter's chin to the light. "What mistake are you talking about? Which one, honey?"

Disentangling from her mother and pushing her hands away, Maggie said, "The only one that matters." With a look that said, *Obviously*, she whispered, "Martin."

"Martin? What are you talking about?"

"I thought I married the anti-dad and instead I did exactly what you did. I married someone I couldn't count on."

"Oh, for heaven's sake. That is utterly ridiculous."

Her mother let Maggie go and searched around for the tie on her chenille robe; finding it dangling, wedged in the back of her slipper, she pulled it forward and fastened it.

"No, it's not! He's home, drunk. Right now."

Laughing at the thought, Maggie's mother said, "He's drunk? Well, I'd have never thought. On second thought, good for Martin."

"Good for Martin? What about me, Mom?"

"Well, you can't drink, honey; you're pregnant. Which is a real shame these days, if you ask me. A little wine really takes the edge off. Sit down. Tell me what's going on." She ushered her daughter into her living room and guided her onto the oatmeal-colored velvet couch. "First the doctor's appointment. Which, mind you, I totally understand, but now this. It's after midnight. You should be in bed. You look remarkably good for coming up on nine months, but you must be exhausted."

"I am, Mom. I'm exhausted."

"Did you make another doctor's appointment?"

"No, but I will." Placing both hands on her belly, she massaged it lovingly. "The baby is doing really well. I can feel her swimming around in there. She's nocturnal, I think. Sometimes, she's up all night. Nighttime is my favorite."

"I'm going to make you some hot chocolate. Tell me what happened." Her mother walked over to the stove.

"He played softball all night, then got wasted when the team won."

Her mother's skeptical look gave Maggie renewed venom.

"One of the reasons I married him was because he was a total loser at sports."

"Really? I don't remember that in the vows."

"After we were engaged, we visited his parents in the house he grew up in. In Martin's old bedroom there weren't any brass trophies of young men in batting stance or deflated footballs anywhere. Instead, on his bulletin board, next to a ticket stub from the Smithsonian, were two blue ribbons from a solo and ensemble band competition."

"So, you're upset that he is playing softball and liking it?"

"Look, I've never been one of those stupid girls longing for bulging muscles and great hand-eye coordination. I know a strong pitching arm does not necessarily translate into good character. I was never deluded that what was useful on the playing field would translate easily to the field of marriage. Daddy taught me that in spades."

Maggie's mind tiptoed to the memory of David, holding the parts to her ceiling fan. She was certain that David was one of those boys in high school who was handsome, confident, and physically gifted—a dangerous threesome of tools given to boys without fluency in how to work the safety.

"Those men should be locked in a gun cabinet for the duration."

"One game and a few beers and you think Martin is Babe Ruth?"

"He's never home."

"Now we're getting somewhere."

"I need help. I can't do this alone."

"Be specific. He can't help you carry this baby. What is he not doing?"

"He's not doing anything. I had to get someone to

help me put the crib together. He works all the time. It's like he's avoiding me."

Maggie's mother considered this. She looked at her daughter's pale and tired face. "While it might be widely known that I am not an expert, I will say this: A problem in your marriage is not a problem marriage and a beer with the buddies is not budding alcoholism."

"He's never home," Maggie repeated.

"Maggie Elizabeth, you are whining like a child, and it's you who isn't home right now."

"Mom!"

"Oh, stop it. Drink your cocoa and either stay the night or go home." Her mother took a deep breath through her nose and said, "You are very pregnant; your husband is at your house right now. He's a good man and you are not an easy woman."

Maggie stood to confront her mother. "I can't believe you just said that."

"Listen, Maggie. Martin couldn't be more different than your father if he was an orangutan. Don't you remember how enthusiastic and sweet he was when you were planning the wedding? He was up for anything. You were the one who was going to decorate your own cake and sculpt your likenesses in butter."

Maggie sighed at the memory and some of her anxiety flittered out between her lips and scattered around the room. "It's not enough, Mom. It's all"—she tried to find the words—"skimming confection, when what I need is infrastructure."

Her mother gently steered her to the front door and nudged her outside, back into the well-lit hall. "Go home," she said, and with the comfort foods of syrup and frosting in her voice, she added, "Maggie, remember, he lost a child, too."

As Maggie walked toward her car, she heard the door reopen. "PS, make another doctor's appointment and I'll meet you there," her mother whispered.

Maggie stood over Martin, his head in what looked like an uncomfortable position on the floor, knees tucked up, snoring. She shook her head and retrieved a crocheted throw from the couch. She gently placed it on Martin and folded it around his torso, being careful not to wake him.

She climbed into bed, the hood of her raincoat cradling her hair. She admitted to herself that she was preoccupied by a new unpredictable person. The volley, the pass, the deflection of intimacy. And as she drifted off to sleep, she had a new appreciation for the jocks of high school and their fascination with the touchdown, the successful completion of a fully vigilant, consistent system. Something she knew she had never had herself.

## *Big Titus*

Standing in the checkout line at Vegetable Medley, the organic grocery in the center of town, Maggie arched her back and rubbed her eyes. She openly considered the lovely soft-figured woman with gray hair and daisy earrings standing in front of her. The woman wore a matching outfit of light blue faux denim with white topstitching and elastic at all stress points. Maggie gazed at the woman's buttocks—a large pair of soft pillows—exactly the right amount of firmness for neck support, yet cushioning enough for true pleasure. Maggie thought if she could just rest her head right there, on this woman's bottom, she might get the real rest she needed.

What was wrong with her lately? She was forever sleeping or wanting to sleep when she needed to do something or was wide-awake when she couldn't do a thing. Last night was an example of both. Thank God she had gotten out of the house before Martin was off the treadmill this morning.

As she leaned heavily on the cold metal of the shopping cart, her eyes filtered across the front page of a newspaper in a wire holder next to various gums and mints. "Baby Gets Ride of Her Life." Peering more closely, she read about a young mother who, while unlocking her car door, placed her child, in her portable car seat, onto the roof of her car like a soda can. Forgetting the child, she snapped the door shut, clipped her own seatbelt into place, and accelerated. The story went on to report that the woman drove several blocks on a straightaway, signaled, slowed slightly, and turned. Continuing on its own trajectory, the car seat flew from atop the sedan, through the air, and landed in the grassy boulevard. Maggie straightened and lifted the newspaper in apprehension. The reporter proclaimed the child uninjured—shaken and crying, but ultimately without a scratch. The article went on with a small ovation for durable car seats, proper installation, and a cautionary word about sleep deprivation and post-partum depression. Then came the big finish, the simple words every mother reading the article held her breath for: "No charges were filed in the incident."

*There by the grace of God go I*, thought Maggie.

It was probably momentarily thrilling for the child: the movement of the car, the wind rushing over her swaddled body, even the sailing sensation as the car banked and the airborne seat continued on course. But surely the pavement was a terrible shock. A hard lesson to learn at such a tender age: What goes up must come down.

*Enjoy the moment, honey, 'cause the comedown ain't no weekend in Paris*, Maggie thought. *Parenting lesson number one.*

Dropping the newspaper back onto the shelf, she glanced around for someone to share her wisdom with. Maggie smiled and locked eyes with the checker holding her cilantro. Before Maggie could speak the woman said, "Paper or plastic and is this parsley?"

Maggie swiped at a piece of hair that fell loose from her ponytail and placed her groceries on the conveyer belt, watching as the orange juice hypnotically followed her frozen peas toward the cashier. "Plastic and yes." Changing her mind she said, "No, paper, I think. And that isn't parsley; it's that other stuff. It's flatter and tastes kind of soapy."

The woman rung into the cash register the price for a bundle of parsley.

"I'm sorry. I'm a little foggy this morning."

The woman shrugged and said, "We get a lot of that."

Maggie smiled gratefully and quickly paid, sheepishly taking her bag of groceries and saying, "Cilantro. It's cilantro," to no one in particular.

Knocking her hand against a large cooler of sodas, the sound of her wedding ring scraping the glass startled her and she shook her head. She seemed to be losing steam. Like a balloon, she had started high and proud but now was only able to hover a foot or two off the floor. Outside, she started her van. Grasping the gearshift, she hesitated, swiftly undid her seatbelt, shoved the car door open with her shoulder, and boosted herself up to retrieve her wallet from the roof of the car.

At that moment, she seriously considered giving up the nighttime vandalizing altogether. But Maggie was a member of the clean-your-plate, finish-what-you-started club, and she didn't wash her hands of a task until the fork scraped across and screeched, "Enough!"

Thank goodness there were other ways to harass people beyond showing up on their front lawns and breaking off the postman flag on the mailbox. Maggie ticked through the list in her head as she drove home. She had sent *Cat Fancy* and *Budget Travel* magazine subscriptions to the Tyson house, had pizzas delivered, called the Church of Jesus Christ of Latter-Day Saints requesting a visit, and canceled all newspaper deliveries. Maybe she should think up something new for today, something that might force a reaction. Then she wondered, *Did she want a reaction?*

She slowed as she approached Tyson's house, taking in the appealing bungalow. On her first visit, she had expected a drab, clapboard ranch with a dog kennel and dead poinsettias left over from Christmas. Today she noticed that someone had planted a tree where Maggie had dumped the bleach a few nights ago. The trunk spindle supported by fresh dirt piled around the base looked like a picket sign against intrusion, the shovel a warning. Her eyes darted over the property looking for signs of life, hoping to catch the felon doing something felonious. But the birds sang dutifully, clearly oblivious, and the neighborhood fairy tale continued.

There was a sudden movement at the corner of her eye, and Maggie simultaneously slammed the brake to the floor and braced herself for impact. Her car tires screeched as they gripped the asphalt and a flurry of CDs previously held in her overhead visor crashed into the windshield. She heard her watermelon roll and thud against the plastic hub that held her spare tire in the back of the van. Cringing, with her sunglasses askew and hanging from one ear, she opened her eyes to survey the damage. A fat, black-and-white cat stood its ground against Maggie's van. Her outraged and indignant expression said, "Bring it on, bitch." Lifting her tail, she turned and strolled away with a yowl that was the feline equivalent of "I never!"

Without looking back, Maggie accelerated away from the scene, hoping she hadn't called too much attention to herself. She drove slowly the rest of the way home and steered the car carefully up her driveway. She had to sort out these ping-ponging emotions and plans. If she didn't iron out the pleats in her brain, she would be too spacey, too wishy-washy to care for a baby. And the baby, she reminded herself, was the point of everything.

Carrying her groceries, knowing Martin would be at work, she trudged into the kitchen where the clock on the stove practically shouted with exasperation: 9:57.

Another morning wasted to this fog she couldn't clear. She flicked on the light, which made the overhead ceiling fan whirr. On the countertop, she saw a note from Martin: *I'm sorry. We need to talk*. Crumpling the note, she pushed Play and listened to her answering machine.

"Shit. Where are you? How many porn queens does it take to change a lightbulb? If you want to know, call me." The clatter of Julia's impatient hang-up came through the tiny plastic speaker followed by the answering machine's beep.

Next, her mother's voice came on the line. "Let me know when you've rescheduled your doctor's appointment. We'll go to lunch and talk."

Maggie closed her eyes with fatigue.

Then David's voice sprang forward and Maggie opened her eyes.

"Maggie? Hi, this is David . . . I, uh, I'm calling . . . How's the fan?" He gave a self-conscious half laugh and continued, "I just thought if you didn't have plans, you might like to go to an auction in Pardeeville. Don't you love the name of that town? . . . Yo, Par-tay-ville. Uh, anyway, the auction lists some first edition books I'm interested in, so I thought I'd go check it out. My mom has to work. So I thought my pregnant, married friend might like to go. So . . . I'm leaving around twelve thirty. Call if you wa—" The answering machine beeped again, cutting off his last word. *If I want*, she thought. She pushed the button and listened again, and then again. *Friend*, she thought. *Am I that? What am I? No. Maybe. A friend doesn't fantasize about another's muscular forearms.* She dialed. He answered on the first ring.

"David, it's Maggie. Pick me up on the way. I'll be ready."

Her lethargy gone, Maggie sprang into action. She called Martin and left a message at work. "Hi, honey. Sorry I missed you this morning. I'm sorry, too. I'll see you tonight for dinner. Should we order Chinese?" This was not enough, she knew, but she would make amends, pay more attention, be a better wife.

Then she noticed another note on the bulletin board

from Martin that she had somehow missed earlier: *Beverly called. Biking? Surveillance duties?*

"What now," breathed Maggie. She threw both notes in the trash. She wouldn't have time for a shower and maybe that would be good. She didn't want David to think she was getting ready, primping for him.

Dialing Julia, she let the phone ring the usual four times then waited through the familiar answering machine message: "Say hi to the Morrises and then get off the phone. It's too nice to be inside calling us." Julia was a pathologic screener and never answered her phone. "I've got a finite amount of 'nice' in me," she would say. "I'm not going to waste it on a telemarketer. I may need it for my in-laws or when the police call wanting to arrest me for my cat-at-large."

"It's me," Maggie said. "Pick up." She heard the scuttle of the phone in the headset as Julia fumbled with the receiver.

"How am I ever going to get this bod in shape if you continue to cancel our morning workouts without so much as a phone call?" Julia said.

"I couldn't get out of bed, and then I had to run to the store," said Maggie.

"Doing some late night biking, are you?"

"No." She started to say more, but Julia budged in like a bully in the hot-lunch line.

"I'm hoping you've gotten it out of your system before you become the neighborhood disgrace."

"All right, you've made your point. I'm calling to tell you we'll have to walk tomorrow. I'm going to an auction today."

"You are? Cool. Who are you going with?" There was a pause and Julia said, "Not with David. You're not going with David, are you?"

"I've never been to an auction, but I've always wanted to."

Julia didn't speak right away, and then said, "This is what I think we should do. Let's go to a spa for the weekend. We'll get a pedicure, drink some Virgin Bloody Marys, and schedule a massage with a really beautiful male masseur."

"What are you talking about?"

"Whenever I start getting bored with Big Steven, I get a massage at the Palms and Pearls Day Spa. I pretend I am having an affair with a particularly gifted man, who I haven't yet slept with, and who is trying to impress me with his dexterity and collection of oils. I have the whole fantasy in my head, and I come home with a much-improved attitude and a renewed interest in a husband-facilitated orgasm. I consider it foreplay. Elaborate and expensive, yes; but it's better than the push-pull-click-click my husband invests in, believe me. Plus, it puts the seven-year itch off for another month or two."

"I am not thinking of having an affair. I'm pregnant. No one in their right mind would want a pregnant woman as a plaything and, frankly, my body will not be affair-ready for a long time."

Julia clucked her tongue. "You want to hear the latest news from camp crazy?"

"Yeah, but keep it short."

"Mikey was on the Internet yesterday supposedly doing a report on great white sharks. So, when I went to check my email later on, I had all this porn spam popping up all over the place. I went up to the dropdown menu and between the great white shark sites were a bunch of attempts to find 'big titties!' Except, God bless his learning disability, Stevie didn't know how to spell it, and it kept coming up with a clarification page: 'Did you mean big titus?' over and over again. Can you imagine his frustration? Here he is trying to find some big-breasted cheerleaders and all he can get is a spelling lesson."

Maggie snorted. "I can't believe *you* are giving *me* life advice. You can bet when this baby comes I won't be calling for your Dr. Seuss–like philosophies on childrearing."

"I'm here to help, honey, just a phone call away." And then Julia added, "Listen, Maggie, be careful."

"I promise to be careful," sighed Maggie. "Unfortunately, *careful* is my middle name."

# *Happily Ever After*

Sitting in the diner's bathroom, Maggie pictured David patiently waiting at their table for two just a few feet away. She looked around the tiny restroom and wondered if she could rent it out by the hour. It had a calm, uncomplicated feel to it, only a few options to explore here. There was an extra toilet paper roll on the back of the tank camouflaged in a white crocheted poodle outfit, the crazy craft eyeballs rolling and unspecific. A cross-stitched sign hung at eye level above the toilet: *We Aim to Please. You Aim, Too, Please!* with a bull's-eye in red, and white hand-sewn *x*'s. Maggie envisioned the owner proudly displaying her handiwork, thinking of the time she would save with less cleaning to do.

Maggie took a deep breath as she washed her hands, letting the icy water cool the blood rushing up her arms and into her circulatory system. *Hot* and *Cold* were printed on both faucet handles, and she considered for a moment that she, too, must have a hidden bipolar spigot somewhere inside her. *This would explain a lot*, she thought. She was either excited about the baby or alarmed, depending on the time of day. Martin conjured both frank irritation and gentle stability. And David, well, David was a different kind of tug.

If Maggie was honest with herself, David was more about hot-hot rather than hot-cold. She let out a breath, pursed her lips, and blew upward. The fringe of her brown bangs lifted and settled. Maggie repeated this exhalation from various sides of her mouth. First left, then right, and back to center.

In college, she had taken a group dynamics class that focused on conflict. Standing at the front of the room, her professor, Dr. Larson, had written the definition of double approach-avoidance conflict. This, Maggie recalled, was when a person has two different desires, and as the person gets closer to one desire, the craving for the other increases.

With a sly smile, Dr. Larson had said, "The ultimate *need* cha-cha-cha."

"Well, that's just everyday life," Maggie had blurted

out in class all those years ago. And the professor had looked at Maggie, narrowed her eyes kindly, and said, "Well, yes, sort of, but life isn't always filled with conflict."

*When isn't it?* Maggie thought, but didn't say aloud. And right then she knew she could learn nothing practical from Dr. Larson, in her white button-down oxford shirt and her naturally blond hair.

Now Maggie placed her hands at the small of her back and stretched. Stepping into the hallway, she noticed the linoleum was worn out at the threshold of the bathroom, which confirmed the popularity of the room. David smiled as she walked toward their table.

"I thought I'd lost you," he said.

"Oh, I had gum on my shoe," she said without meeting his eyes. "I was trying to pry it lose with a nail file. Apparently, they should use gum on our highways; it's indestructible."

"Good to know," he said, raising his eyebrows as he finished an onion ring.

Maggie took her place next to him in the red plastic booth. Their backs were against the front window, where the name of the restaurant—*Lucy's Dine and Dash*—was lettered in arched script. The aging sign had been commissioned before fast food became popular, making the title an invitation to larceny instead of a quick meal. The Dash, as the Elmwood locals called it, was true to the stereotype of a small-town restaurant. There wasn't a trendy no-smoking section, and the menu featured a nonspecific cold-meat plate and soup special.

Maggie licked her lips. "The auction was fun. Can you believe how much that woman paid for the jumbo bag of Beanie Babies?"

Making a face, David said, "Crazy. I think the box of doorknockers went quickly in the bidding. Who needs that many doorknockers?" A woman cruised toward them with the bowed legs and tight calves of a career waitress. The varicose veins in her legs pulsed with the right to be there, telling tales of long days, lots of miles, and night-time foot soaks. Her nametag read *Judy* in red cursive above her right breast. She placed the bill, torn from her carbon paper pad, between them and said, "Anything else I can get you folks? We make a tasty milkshake."

Maggie shook her head, as she rested her hand on her belly. "I'm stuffed. I think the gravy on the fries did me in."

Judy smiled. "It's homemade," she said. "Not from a jar."

"We're not in Pardeeville anymore. Anything goes," David answered, winking at Maggie.

"You can either bring the bill to the register or leave it set right there," said Judy, reaching for Maggie's plate just as she snatched the last french fry. David sat quietly, fingering his napkin and staring at a spot somewhere in the distance. Maggie cleared her throat and said, "Conversation is weird. It's like walking or breathing. If you don't think about it, you can manage without effort. But if you pay too much attention—right, left, in, out, noun, verb—you wind up tripping and hyperventilating." Then she laughed and said, "I can't think of anything to say."

David shook his head. "I can think of a lot of things, but sometimes it's good to just digest a bit."

Maggie brushed the surface of the metal-rimmed table and picked at a piece of faded silver confetti bonded to the top. They were sitting side by side and spoke to each other in almost a confessional fashion.

"I usually hang out with my girlfriend, Julia, and she can talk herself silly in an empty room. I don't typically have to fill silences," Maggie said.

"Well, you're not in charge of this one." David reached and gave her knee a squeeze, stopped and withdrew his hand. He tried to slow the abruptness of his retreat and ended up with a palsy-like movement.

As if the awkwardness had crossed some bridge toward intimacy, Maggie asked, "Have you ever been engaged before?"

"Nope," he said. "This will be my first."

"Why not? I mean, are you what they call a commitment-phobe?"

"No," he answered tightly, and then softened to say, "You ask that like there are flocks of women sitting around waiting for commitment-ready men." There was a moment of silence before he added, "I don't stay in many places for long."

This admission felt to Maggie like running into someone you dislike at the grocery store. She dropped her eyes and tried to hide herself in the canned goods.

With a tentative look in her direction, David asked quietly, "How did it happen with you and Martin?"

"Oh, I don't know," she said vaguely. "He was in the right place at the right time." Maggie paused. "I don't mean that unkindly. I mean it like it was the blending of lowered resistance and general attraction."

"Well, that's romantic."

"Yeah, well, I . . . romance." Maggie paused and then continued quietly. "When I was a girl, my father used to bet on the horses. 'Don't you love the names of the fillies, my little Mags?' he would say. 'Libber and Onions, Frankoo Verymuch, Heavenly Dreams.' He'd tell me that if he had a horse to race, he would name it Maggie's Magic." Maggie brushed back the hair on her forehead and felt a piece of grit on her fingertips.

"I used to think having a husband was going to be a fairy tale, but now I know it's more like one of my dad's horse races." She put her head back on the booth and breathed out. "Turns out my dad's alcohol and gambling stuff was really a lesson in romance. Maybe everything we learn from our parents is ultimately accidental parenting."

David didn't offer anything like a head nod or a meaningless *I know what you mean.* He just waited, and his silence nudged her on.

"Because of him, I think finding one's true love is a race to the finish with horses named Fat Chance and Happily Ever After. For years, when I was still dating, I could always tell just before things would turn south." Maggie took a drink from a large, ruby red plastic glass and the sound of the clinking ice pushed her to continue. "The guy would forget to call, or make a crude joke at the wrong moment, or do some other all-too-human thing. And I would hear the announcer in my head"—Maggie plugged her nose and mimicked a television announcer—"Happily Ever After is in the lead! Oh, wait, here comes Fat Chance on the inside track. Here he comes, folks, and it's Fat Chance and Happily Ever After, Fat Chance and Happily Ever After, neck and neck!" She chuckled grimly. "Then I would begin to notice tiny things that I didn't like. He chewed funny, or maybe he favored ugly western shirts, and then the race was finished, and it was Fat Chance by a nose." Maggie paused a minute and added, "So, I picked the horse named Going the Distance instead of Prince Charming." Maggie sat up and laughed a weak dismissive laugh and shrugged. "It's like what my mother used to say to me, 'Funny and nice beats handsome and charming every single time,' but I still wonder if she was right about that. Seems to me that handsome and charming can wrestle funny and nice to the ground."

There was the clink of a coffee cup and the whirr of a blender nearby. The cash register rang. "You know," Maggie said, "no matter how hard you try to iron the wrinkles out, you find yourself falling asleep in your best life and waking up creased." The door opened to their right and a man in a plaid short-sleeved shirt and John Deere hat walked in. Maggie raised her eyes and saw that David was looking at her. He gazed at her forehead and then, gently, on her lashes. After a beat, he dropped his eyes to her cheek, finally pausing at her lips. He swallowed hard.

Once, when Maggie was in high school, a stage hypnotist came for an assembly. His name was Johnny Wand, and years later she still thought this name was more pornographic than hypnotic. He stood on stage in front of several of her seated classmates, who slumped together quietly, holding their hands straight out in front of them. Some of their heads lolled to the side in a parody of sleep, and others, more dignified, sat upright, eyes soft and closed. Maggie watched as their hands moved together slowly and magnetically while the hypnotist told them to keep them apart. "Try hard," he said. "Don't let them touch." And with great effort, the students worked to stop the charismatic pull of their hands. Maggie hadn't fully understood the struggle until now feeling the pull toward David knowing she would never bridge the gap between them. She visualized the hurdles between them, as if they had cutout names glued to them: Martin, The Baby, David's Fiancée, Julia—all on the track waiting to be cleared or knocked down.

Gently David reached up and moved a piece of hair behind Maggie's ear. He dropped his fingers to her collarbone and then returned his hand to his lap.

"We'd better get going," he said, placing a twenty-dollar bill on the table. "I've got to get home. Strange things have been happening lately. Someone has been sort of vandalizing our house in the middle of the night, and my mom doesn't like to be home alone in the evenings anymore." And then, noticing the alarm on Maggie's face and wanting to reassure her, he said, "It doesn't really feel malicious. It's more mischievous, like they lop off the heads of our geraniums and drop lawn killer on the grass. It's kind of crazy." As he said this, he turned and slid out of the booth.

## *Giving an Imaginary Predator the Slip*

A smoke alarm went off in Maggie's head. A loud insistent beeping: *Where there's smoke, there's fire!* Her eyes darted to his back as he walked to the door. *Oh, God,* she thought. *I've been vandalizing the wrong house.* She steadied herself as she got out of the booth to follow him. She cleared her throat. "Vandalizing?" she said. "Where do you live, exactly? I can't believe I don't know."

"Over on Hemlock," David replied. "The house with the green shutters. Fifty-six."

With as much nonchalance as she could possibly muster under the circumstances, Maggie asked, "How long have you lived there?"

"A long time. I left in '97, but my folks have been there

for sixteen years." He pushed out the restaurant door and left Maggie standing on the faded linoleum with a lump the size of sixteen years in her throat.

She shoved the heavy glass door open and stepped out into the fading sunshine. David was looking back for her and waited on the curb before opening her car door.

"Maggie, you are looking a little grayish. Are you feeling all right?"

She hid her face with both hands and said, "No, actually. All of a sudden I feel pretty terrible." He started toward her as if to help, but she dropped both hands from her face, held them out defensively and said, too loudly, "No!" David stopped. She recovered enough to stutter out a little nervous laugh and say, "I throw up without warning these days. You'd better stay where you are." She hurried to her side of the car and paused, looking at the door handle. She met David's eyes over the top of the car. "I just don't feel very good. The gravy. Maybe I should call Martin."

Calmly, David spoke, "Maggie, you are fine. Whatever's going on right now will pass. Sit down; we'll put the air conditioner on; we don't even have to talk, but I am driving you safely home."

The heat and the swarming of her thoughts made her want to suddenly sit. Maggie slid into her seat. She kept her seatbelt unbuckled, one hand on the handle and the other spread protectively on her belly. David glanced at her several times as they drove from the center of town to her house.

They didn't speak, but Maggie's brain was firing on all cylinders. She kept seeing flashes of Ella's white body and helpless face. The nurses in Minnesota.

As soon as David pulled up her driveway, she flung the door open and stepped onto the asphalt. Leaning out of the still-moving car, she thrust her weight through the doorway and landed hard on the pavement. David slammed on the brake. "Maggie!" he gasped. She felt pain in her knee and ripped the scab off her hand.

David was halfway around the car when Maggie shouted, "Stay there!" Pulling on the armrest of the open door she stood up. "I'm fine. I just need to get out of the heat."

"You're bleeding. Let me help you." He paused and looked into her eyes. "It's all right," he said more quietly. "It's all right. You're okay."

"I'm embarrassed enough. Just let me get myself together, okay? I need to be alone."

Limping up her front walk, she didn't look back, but fumbled for her cell phone as she unlocked the door. Stepping into her cool living room, she dialed Martin at work, then hung up before he could answer. She dialed again, then slapped her phone shut. What would she say to him, her husband? *David and Craig Tyson are the same man? David, the man I have unexpected feelings for is also the man whose house I have been vandalizing?* She dialed Julia, hung up, and dropped her phone onto the floor. Pacing around her living room, her thoughts flew around her head like gnats gathering speed and bonded together into anxiety that clutched at her chest. Setting her jaw, she raced upstairs to her computer. The Department of Corrections website loaded Tyson's face.

There it was. How had she missed it before? The set of his jaw, the eyes, the now-familiar expression she had missed earlier. It was not sadness, it was a different look. A look that said, *I know something you don't know.*

*Yeah?* she thought now. *Well, not for long, buddy.*

When the telephone rang, Maggie jumped up from behind her desk and ran to the top of the stairs to listen. The answering machine kicked in and Julia's voice wound its way upstairs. "Maggie? Are you home yet? Call me on my cell. We've got to talk." Maggie shoved the door closed and spun on her heel. She grabbed the upstairs telephone extension and slammed it into the docking station. Then she picked it up and slammed it down again, knocking a water glass to the floor. "Dammit."

Holding her head in frustration, Maggie reached for the phone and dialed Martin's number again. But he didn't answer. "What's the use of having a phone if you're never,

ever going to answer it?" she muttered. She hung up and let the headset drop. The floorboards in the hall outside her office creaked, and Maggie sat upright. Her eyes darted first to the door, then to the headset on the floor.

"Who's there?" Her voice clattered in her ears.

The door swung wide and there stood Julia.

"Maggie?" Seeing the look of panic on Maggie's face, Julia looked around the room and said, "What? What's the matter?"

"What the hell are you doing here?" Maggie asked, in a voice that sounded hysterical even to her.

Immediately Julia opened her hands, palms up, and said, "I'm sorry. I didn't mean to scare you. I called from the driveway a minute ago. We got cut off. Your front door was open and I saw your cell phone on the floor. I called out but I guess you didn't hear me. God, honey, I'm sorry."

"Sorry! You're always sorry! You're always so right."

"What?"

"I'm sick of you. I'm sick of Martin, too!"

Julia took a tentative step forward. "What's going on, Maggie?"

"No!" Maggie shouted again. Then more softly, "No, I'm not about to talk to you about it. Little Miss I-Told-You-So. Little Miss I-Have-All-the-Answers. Well, guess what, Julia, some of your answers are wrong."

The weight of Maggie's words fell between them. Somewhere nearby a garbage truck screeched, its metal arm filled with refuse. Julia spoke quietly. "I know. Believe me. I know."

Maggie inhaled through her nose. "I knew. I did, but I ignored it. When I was little, my mom would practice with me. She'd ask me, 'If a man comes by and wants you to help find his kitty, you should do what?' I would say, 'Run away and tell an adult.' Then she'd say, 'If he tries to touch you in your *area of utmost privacy*, what then?' I always knew the answer. 'I'll shout *no* and run the other way!' I always got straight A's in the game of giving an imaginary predator the slip." Maggie shook her head with disdain. "What a joke. It's the real predators I can't identify."

"Did something happen today?"

With a vicious intensity Julia had rarely seen from her best friend, her childhood comrade, Maggie said, "What did you come here for anyway. To gloat?"

"Gloat? About what? No. I—" Her voice faltered and she said, "I'm pregnant. I came to tell you, I'm pregnant." Julia's jaw trembled.

The expression on Julia's face spoke volumes. Her words effectively derailed Maggie's tirade.

"You can probably guess how I feel about it." Julia couldn't meet her friend's eyes. "I know I should be happy, grateful even." She coughed to hide the catch in her throat. "It's just . . . I'm not like you, Maggie. I'm selfish." Julia sat on the cedar chest that she knew held Ella's baby blanket as well as her birth and death certificates. She placed her hand flat on the wood. "My boys are my breath. I'm scared to death to divide that breath into thirds. More kids, more chances for loss." She inhaled, afraid to mention the name of Maggie's baby for fear of resurrecting more pain. "Ella's death, seeing what it did to you. To Martin. It effectively turned me into a frightened coward. I don't want to be a part of your Neighborhood Watch because I don't want to lift my blinders any more than I absolutely have to."

Maggie stared at Julia, whose head was bowed, her chin tucked in the way a child's might be after having been caught lighting a match.

Julia spoke softly. "You're the courageous one. You've always been the one willing to stick your neck out." She touched her abdomen. "Don't be mad at me. I'm going to need you."

Maggie stood and moved over to her best friend, the girl who had stood by her through every event in her life. She took Julia's hand. "I'm so sorry. I've been such a jerk," Maggie said.

## *Tyson/D the P*

Maggie knelt by the green Honda sedan, holding the blunt end of her favorite tweezers to the tire valve. The hissing sound mingled with the occasional croak of a bullfrog and a halfhearted dog bark, and it was accompanied by a sniggering of guilt that rolled around in her thoughts. A pleasant breeze ruffled her hair. "Another beautiful night for defacing property," she whispered to herself, gritting her teeth with effort.

Shifting her position slightly, she negotiated around her belly and lifted her leg to shoo away a pebble at her kneecap. Flexing her fist to release the cramp in her hand, she reconsidered her plan to deflate all four tires.

*He'll get the point*, she thought.

She glanced up at the house and wondered which room belonged to Tyson/David the Predator. She liked the new nickname she had thought up; it fit him now that she knew who he was. Tyson/D the P, the ultimate "rap" artist. She pushed harder. The windows were shut, but still she could hear the hum of the air conditioner.

Lace curtains hung undisturbed in the window facing the street. That must be Tyson/D's mother's room; she doubted *he* favored frilly curtains. Maggie imagined him sleeping in his childhood room a baseball trophy a dusty Model-T.—superhero curtains and a dinosaur lamp. A twin bed, the covers wrapped around his legs, arms flung wide. Unprotected. What if he saw her outside flattening his tires? What would he do? Would he call the police or come to confront her? She pictured his face, livid and hurt.

*What do you think you're doing?* he might say. *What the hell do you think you're doing?*

And she would say, *What the hell do you think* you're *doing, living here? Like some innocent person trying to forget about your past. Making friends with unsuspecting women. What were you planning? Was my baby going to be your next victim?* She would lift her chin and stand her ground. *People like you should just take your charm and easy words and live in a community of other insincere, malevolent shitheads and leave the rest of us alone. Leave* me *alone*, she would say. *I was happy and normal, and then you showed up.*

She grunted with exertion and flashed for a moment to a long-forgotten memory. She had been a girl of seven or so. The night was like this one, calm and filled to the brim with summer. She lay in bed on top of her blanket and felt the window fan feebly blowing warm air into the room. She liked to buzz into the fan, listening to her vibrating robot voice: *Take me to your leader*. Or she would sing in a warbling robin's voice: *Mr. Sandman, bring me a dream. Make him the cutest that I've ever seen.*

She had been so intent on her song that she hadn't noticed the car drive up, but she heard the door slam. Her father was standing at the curb, a duffel bag at his side, his quiet, constant companion. Maggie crept to the top of the stair rail outside her room and watched as he walked in the front door. She hadn't seen him for several months, and he looked worn and frayed, like her favorite stuffed animal, thin with use.

"No," she heard her mother say as he placed his arms around her neck. "Why can't you just leave us alone? We're fine without you."

Maggie wanted to shout, *Don't listen! She doesn't mean it!* But she saw it wasn't necessary. Her mother didn't move from his embrace as she spoke.

She shook her head with the memory and released the

pressure on the tire. She hadn't known how much air a tire held until now. *Learn something new every day*, she thought. Standing, she twisted to the side, stretching her back, when suddenly she heard someone whisper her name. She stopped, waited, and heard it again.

"Maggie!" It was spoken with a hissed urgency. *Tyson-D?* She swiveled her head and spotted Martin, hunched at the side of the driveway.

"Maggie, what in God's name?"

Maggie stared disbelieving at her husband and turned back to the car, repositioning her tweezers.

"Stop it," he whispered and grabbed her arm.

"Go home." Maggie wrenched her arm free and moved her body between the tire and Martin.

"What are you doing?"

She stopped and looked at him. "I think you can see what I'm doing, so either wait while I finish this and walk me home, or stop talking."

"I'm not going to stand here and watch you do this. Christ, it's a good thing Julia called me. Let's go."

This stopped Maggie and she looked up. "Julia called you? Damn her. What'd she tell you?"

"Oh, not much," Martin started casually. "Just that my pregnant wife was outside in the middle of the night, damaging property and probably committing a felony."

Maggie shook her head and scowled at her husband's

frantic face. "Could you lower your voice? This is no more than a misdemeanor at best. I'm just leaving a message." Maggie trudged over to another tire.

Martin moved around the car, trying to cut her off. "I suppose I'm partially to blame here. If I'd been paying attention, I would have listened when Beverly Finker tried to tell me the same thing."

"Beverly called? When? What could she have possibly said?"

"A few days ago. I left you a note. I thought she was the crazy one."

Maggie turned suddenly to face her husband. "Quiet down!" she said in a stage whisper. "Let's go. I guess I'm done here."

"I don't want to rush you. I just thought before someone called the cops I might save your butt. Why are you doing this?"

"Why don't you call Julia if you're so hot to know and she's so willing to tattle?" With renewed outrage, she pulled her bike away from the birch tree it leaned against and moved to the sidewalk. When she turned to look back at Martin, he simply stood next to the listing car. Both of them looked deflated and confused.

Watching her move away, he hurried to catch up, shouting as loud as his whisper would allow. "Is that what I need to do these days? Is that it? God forbid *you* tell me what's going on in that exhausting brain of yours. I have to talk to Julia or David or whoever else seems to know you better than I do—because I sure as hell know you aren't talking to me."

"David? *David?* Why would you talk to him? He doesn't know me, and I sure as heck don't know him."

"Since you're standing in his driveway in the middle of the night, clearly he means more to you than just being our handyman."

Maggie stopped and shoved her bicycle into the street. It clattered to the ground in an undignified heap of handlebars and spokes. She turned on Martin, furiously pointing her finger.

"You knew! You knew that was David's house?"

Irritated, Martin said, "Yeah, I picked him up for softball once. So what?"

"Did you also know that David is a sex offender? Apparently he goes by Craig Tyson when he's breaking the law, and David Johnson when he's playing handyman."

Shaking his head, Martin grimaced. "Don't be ridiculous. He's not a sex offender," then added, "He's on my team," as if this fact proved his innocence.

Maggie widened her eyes. "Well, then he's a softball-playing sex offender," she said. "At least according to the Department of Corrections, he is." The triumph on her face was short-lived and changed quickly to despair. "He *is* a sex offender. He's *the* sex offender." Maggie pulled the shirt of her pajamas up and wiped her face. The streetlight shone from above, exposing the dome of her belly and a grimy face, wet from tears. She kicked the tire of her bike.

The sight of her glowing white belly and anxious face swept away Martin's flimsy mist of anger. He picked up her bike. With his free arm, he reached out for her shoulders. "Mags, what are you talking about? Slow down and tell me what's going on."

Fatigue and frustration flattened Maggie and she looked into Martin's eyes and said, "How am I ever going to keep this baby safe? I can't figure out who the good guys are."

"Yes, you can. You married one. Start at the beginning. I won't get mad, and I promise I'm not going anywhere."

Maggie glanced over her shoulder before she spoke. "David, our handyman, my friend"—she paused at this and made a smirk with her lips before she continued—"your teammate, is listed on the Wisconsin Sex Offender Registry as Craig Tyson, and ten years ago he was found guilty of secondary sexual assault. He looked really different then. I couldn't tell from the photograph that it was him."

Like a cat skating on slick floors, the words slid out of her quickly and without control. "I thought, at first, that I had the wrong house or person, but I went back online and there he was, those same eyes. You know that crooked tooth right in the front of his mouth? There it was, plain as day. I don't know how I didn't see it. The D is his middle name—David—and, turns out, mine is dumb-ass."

She stopped talking for a minute and adjusted her slipper but quickly straightened when she felt her child deep inside of her, a bird's wing of a feeling, a stuttering, a humming buzz. She stood and put her hand on her tummy and waited as if she were straining to hear something.

"Mags?"

"Shhh, wait. Here." And she took his hand and placed it on her stomach.

"I don't feel anything."

Maggie looked at him, and said, "It's the baby. She's always up at night."

Martin looked up, concentrating as if he was trying to remember the capital of Paraguay or the lyrics to a song. After a minute, he placed his arm around Maggie and pulled her in. He kissed the top of her head and said, "Let's get you and this baby home. We need to talk about all of this. But not until we've had some rest." Martin pulled the bike off the ground and turned the tires toward home. She wilted into his body and slipped her hand into his back pocket, her slippers making a scuffing sound all the way home.

* * *

David Johnson is Craig Tyson. The same Craig Tyson who you saw online? Am I getting this right?"

Maggie nodded, wrapping her bathrobe around her even though the bedroom air felt thick and sticky. She closed her eyes and waited for the question.

"What did he do?"

"I haven't any idea." They were sitting, facing each other on the bed, and Maggie closed her eyes. "Let's go to the computer. I'll show you." She had the grayish pall that Martin associated with Ella's death. The bloodless reaction of Maggie's complexion to stress.

"No, not tonight. I believe you. I just need to know a couple of things, and then we should get some rest. When did you figure it out? That this Craig Tyson is the David we know?"

"Yesterday. After the auction, we were talking and he said someone had been doing some"—she paused and cleared her throat, refusing to meet Martin's eye—"things, you know, vandalizing things, and I realized right then that either I had the wrong person or that he *was* the person."

"What things, Mags? How many *things*?"

Maggie twisted her wedding ring. "A few. For the last

three weeks, I've been going there personally or sending something annoying to his address."

"What?" Suddenly angry Martin swore. "Jesus Christ, if anything had happened to you, Maggie. That son-of-a-bitch. If he had touched you . . ."

Maggie saw David's face in the diner, felt his fingertips on her collarbone. She shivered. "It's over now. It's done."

Martin took Maggie into his arms and kissed her lips. "My girl. I should have known. I was working too hard, not paying attention." With a guilty look he added, "Like usual."

The stress of her secret, thoughts of David, and the silence surrounding it all left her like an evil spirit abandoning its host. She stretched her neck forward and said, "What now?"

"I need to know everything."

"Tonight?"

"All I need to know tonight is that you are okay. If you are, then let's go to sleep and talk about this tomorrow." Slapping his forehead, he said, "Shit, I have a staff meeting first thing tomorrow." He took Maggie's hands and said, "It's going to take some time for me to not work as much. I have to get out of a few things, but I will."

"I'm okay," she whispered. "The emergency is over. We'll talk as soon as you get home."

Reassured, he rested his head back, and before long she

could hear his steady deviated-septum snoring. Maggie shook her head. Nobody could stop, drop, and drool like Martin, even during a veritable tornado. Unlike Maggie, who crept slowly out of bed. She slunk into the bathroom, lit only by her seashell nightlight, and eased open the vanity drawer to pull out her green spiral stenographer's pad. The tile floor was cool and smooth on her bare feet.

She often had a brainstorm while showering or brushing her teeth, and there her pad would sit, like an attentive assistant, waiting to record her thoughts. There was something about grooming that inspired her. Maybe it was the Zen-like concentration it took to get the arch right in her eyebrow or to get every last dead, pore-clogging cell during exfoliation. It was in this very upstairs bathroom where she had first imagined taking charge of the Neighborhood Watch. Of course, the meeting hadn't been quite as successful as she had visualized, but really, what is? *Eyebrow arch to boardroom meeting, nothing ever goes as planned.*

She sat on the edge of the tub, pushed the shower curtain aside, and rested her back on the corner of the chilly wall. Using her old bubble script from high school, glossy windows added for dimension to the bloated letters, she scribbled a to-do list: *(1) Get control of life; (2) Be nice to Martin; (3) Do not call Julia when mad; (4) Do something about Beverly; (5) Forget everything about Tyson/David; (6) Plant mums.*

*It's good to live a balanced life*, she thought reasonably, and snapped the notebook shut.

Padding quietly back to bed, she eased herself next to Martin. Still asleep, he rolled onto his side and faced Maggie. His lips were pulled to the bed with a mixture of gravity and relaxation, like the lid on a teapot sliding off the grooves of the top. Maggie considered the possibility that Martin might be the love of her life and pinched his nose. His mouth popped open and his sandpaper snoring ceased.

## *Rock, Paper, Asshole*

Maggie blinked at the leafy sunshine that caressed her blanketed figure. Martin's side of the bed was already empty. *It's a beautiful day*, Maggie thought, wide-awake now, *a beautiful day to take charge of your life.* Her mother would say, *Every morning you get to start all over, a clean slate. Imagine the possibilities.*

*Just imagine*, Maggie thought.

The glowing numbers on the bedside clock read 9:15 a.m. Closing her eyes, she again pictured the look on David's face in the diner. The way he had reached to her, smiled, joked, listened intently. David's warm-faced smile floated before her eyes and was replaced with Tyson's bearded, younger version from the website. Maggie rubbed her face.

"Just let it go," she said aloud.

Pulling herself out of bed and into the kitchen, she read Martin's note: *Didn't want to wake you. Call me.* Maggie dialed his cell instead of his office number, knowing he wouldn't pick up and she could leave a message.

"Honey, I feel good. I'm going out for a walk. I'll pick up your shirts from the cleaners today, and we can have pizza for dinner tonight. We'll talk then. Don't worry." Then as an afterthought, she added, "I love you." This would not sound much like an apology to the casual listener, but Martin would know. She hated pizza. If this wasn't an obvious love note, she didn't know what was. Maggie checked off number two on her list: *Be nice to Martin.*

She pushed open the front door and took a deep breath. After a block of focused, purposeful power walking, she caught sight of Julia, moving toward her, arms pumping. Maggie turned up the volume on her iPod and picked up her pace.

"Maggie! God dammit, wait." Julia was at her elbow gently grabbing her arm.

"Maggie," she said again, and then placed herself directly in front of her friend's path.

"Go to hell," Maggie said, not meeting Julia's eyes and trying to move around her.

Julia put her hands on Maggie's shoulders. "I can explain."

"No, I don't think you can. You're a know-it-all, for sure, but I thought at the very least you were trustworthy. I was wrong. You're Vicky Schumaker from third grade all over again."

Insulted, Julia said, "I am not."

"I told her that I had a crush on Billy Barton, and she ran right over and told him. Do you see the connection? Vicky told Billy, you told Martin. I mean, what the hell is it with you people? Didn't you ever hear the phrase 'loose lips sink ships'? My ship is sinking, again, thanks to you.

"I have nothing to do with your ship sinking this time. You were acting so strangely yesterday. I was worried."

"So you called my 'daddy,' is that it? I'm a grown woman now. You don't have to take care of me anymore, *and* you don't call the shots. I can't believe you sent Martin after me."

"If it were me, you'd have done exactly the same thing. And you know it."

Maggie quieted suddenly, and Julia took the opportunity to ask, "What did Martin do?"

"What do you think he did? He came and got me, and he wants some kind of explanation. Assurances."

"And?" Julia said it quietly, with the fight seeping out of her.

"I don't really know, do I? And now I don't have anyone to talk to about it because my best friend can't keep her trap shut. I guess I'll go try and find some kind of twelve-step program. 'Hello, my name is Maggie and I stalk predators.' There must be somewhere I can admit to my addiction, someplace where confidentiality is actually honored."

"Come off it." Julia's anger flared again. "If I was heading toward a disaster sign, I'd sure as hell hope you would intervene on my behalf."

"So, you're the saintly friend and I'm the crazy, pregnant lady in this scenario, is that right? Did you and Martin have a nice patronizing conversation about hormones and nutty behavior on my behalf? Thanks, but no thanks. I don't need your level-headed advice here or in my marriage."

"Someone needed to do something. What you were doing was against the law, and you could have landed in the newspaper or in jail. Not to mention the baby!"

"Like it isn't against the law when you have a few drinks with your book group and drive home? Or when you bought that gown from Nordstrom for the Black and White Ball and then conveniently returned it? Thanks for the lesson in law. Takes one felon to know one." Maggie added, "Stop trying to take care of me. You suck at it."

"Then stop needing it. And take a different fucking route for a change." They stared at each other, facing off. Maggie's chin was out and Julia had the look of someone about ready to take a swing. The strains of Meatloaf's "Bat Out of Hell" jutted into the air between them, but Julia didn't flinch as she tried to ignore the ring of her cell phone. When the phone hit the chorus, Julia rolled her eyes and flipped her phone open. With frustration and irritation wrapped around her vowels she said, "Hello. What?"

"Julia. Where's Little Steven?"

"What do you mean, 'Where's Little Steven'? He should be with you."

"I can't find him."

She looked at her watch. "What the hell are you talking about?"

"I went to the community building to pick him up from safety camp."

Interrupting her husband, she said, "He's at day camp at the high school, Jesus Christ."

"No, I know that now. I'm at the high school. Nobody's here."

Maggie saw the change in Julia, identified hysteria coming on like a freight train.

Julia started walking away from Maggie. Down the street. Toward her house.

"Where is he, Steven?"

"I don't know. I looked everywhere."

"Listen to me. Go to the front doors of the school and

then take the quickest route home. Maybe he walked. Go!"

Without waiting for a response, she began a jog that turned into a full-out sprinter's run. Maggie followed her, walking as fast as she could.

As she rounded the corner to her neighborhood, Julia scanned the streets. A little blond head. Anywhere. She thought of the online site. The addresses. *What if he's scared?* she thought. *What if he's wondering where his mama is?*

She felt a gob of panic jam up her throat and surge forward. Julia ran down the block, across two lawns, and up to her front door. She already had her hand in her pocket trying to wrestle out the house key. Ripping her pocket, she thrust the key into the lock and shoved the door open. Her breath came in gasps as she strode into her house calling her son's name with forced calm.

"Stevie?"

Mr. Tubby raced by, and with more intensity, Julia called out, "Steven?"

Without breaking stride, she rushed through the hallway to her son's room. She shouldered his door open and scanned it. The sound of glass breaking forced Julia to turn and head into the kitchen, calling, "Steven Bagle Morris! Is that you?"

When she saw him sitting on the counter, chocolate

smeared under the bridge of his nose and on his neck, she shouted, "Why didn't you say something?"

Gulping, her son said, "You always say to swallow your food before talking."

She bent at the hip, trying to catch her breath. After a moment, she rushed to hug him. Cupping the back of his head, she held him fast and breathed in his scent. French-fried potatoes and hair in need of a wash—an odor that conjured well-being such that the Dalai Lama has never known.

Trying to wriggle free, Little Steven pointed to the broken glass on the floor of the kitchen. "I broke the lid to the cookie jar. Are you mad?"

"No, baby." Feeling her throat constrict, she swallowed hard and said, "How'd you get home?"

"Mrs. Talbert gave me a ride. I used the garage code. I had to stand on my bike. Mrs. T waited until I got inside."

"Did you tell her your daddy was coming?"

"No. I wanted to get home. I was starving to death."

Wild-eyed, Steven pounded up the porch stairs and into the house.

"You found him. Thank God."

Julia trained a scathing look at her husband. "No thanks to you."

Little Steven pushed free of his mother and jumped off the kitchen counter. Handing his father a cookie, he said,

"Hey, Dad. Where ya been?" Not waiting for an answer, he scuttled down the hallway to his room calling for Mr. Tubby.

Julia stabbed a look at Big Steven. "Yeah, *Dad.* Where ya been?"

He wiped his hand over his face. "It was an honest mistake."

"An honest mistake is forgetting to put your gas cap back on. This is neglect. If you were my babysitter, I'd fire you."

Maggie banged her way inside the house. "Did you find him?"

Steven rounded on her. "This whole thing is your fault. This would be nothing if you and your sex offender would get out of our lives."

Maggie dropped her jaw and the color drained from her face. She looked like a fish gasping for air.

Julia shouted, "Oh, no you don't. You are not going to pass this off on Maggie. Safety camp was ages ago. He's been going to day camp for three weeks. Three weeks! Do you think you could possibly keep up?"

Steven looked first at one woman, then the other. "If Maggie hadn't come along talking about perverts, you would not be reacting this way. You'd have laughed before."

"That may be, Steven. But I would have been wrong to laugh. Dead wrong."

Julia stepped over the broken lid on the kitchen floor and pulled her husband into the garage. She slammed the door behind them.

Maggie had a stricken look on her face, a hand on her belly, and a misting of perspiration on her upper lip. She glanced around the room. There were wet swimsuits hanging from doorknobs and towels flung in the entryway to the mudroom. She stepped around a pair of underwear and what looked like a half-eaten peanut butter sandwich but could have been a doggie treat. Artwork covered the cabinets both high and low, and there was an old egg-crate sculpture of a tomato or tonsil or blood clot on the round wooden kitchen table.

She listened to Julia's and Steven's voices as they hissed and snapped through the weather seal, sneaking in around the molding like a frost. The couple's anger morphed into relief as they realized what had been narrowly avoided—the end of their happy lives as they had known them.

Maggie heard Steven drive away as Julia emerged from the garage.

"I felt like crap today and didn't want to pick up the kids from camp and swimming. I asked Big Steven to help, just this once. I should have been clearer. Y'know, about where Little Stevie was." Julia bent to pick up the broken cookie jar lid. "It didn't go so well out there." She gestured to the garage with her head. "He said he hadn't felt that great today, either. To give him a break for screwing up. I told him that suffering from acute assholishness did not trump general malaise and best-friend betrayal. He told me to stop being so dramatic. I challenged him to a duel of rock, paper, asshole, and it went downhill from there."

Maggie looked at her friend with admiration. "How'd you know Stevie would be in the house?" she asked.

"God, I didn't. He knew how to get inside in case of an emergency. I just hoped."

Maggie shook her head. "I can see how Big Steven would blame me."

Julia shrugged in partial agreement. "I *have* been worried about you. I saw you bike by my house last night and knew I had to do something. Big Steven was out of town, and I couldn't leave the boys alone in the house and go after you myself. Incidentally, I don't think the Neighborhood Watch is exactly working like you expected. It appears that I'm the only one on the lookout, and I'm not even an official member."

"Oh, I know. Those losers. Don't forget Beverly, though. She's turned out to be a real trooper."

Julia looked puzzled.

"Beverly called Martin."

Julia swept up the rest of the broken glass and dumped it into the trash.

"There's more to all of this," Maggie said. "You don't know the best part. My new friend David is actually Tyson the Predator. The man whose house I have been visiting at night is also the man I've been spending my days with."

Julia inhaled sharply and said, "What the hell?"

Maggie laughed a bitter laugh. "I don't know. Coincidence, fate, or just my usual luck, but there it is. My crush and my nemesis are one and the same."

Then, to Maggie's great surprise, Julia's eyes filled with tears. But although her eyes waved the white flag, her jaw was still clenched tight as a fist. Trying to maintain control she said, "Oh, my God. If anything had happened to Little Steven . . ." Julia staggered a little at the thought. "I'm sorry." One tear snaked out of her eye and scooted to safety under her chin. "I just can't do this anymore."

Maggie sat at her best friend's kitchen table. It occurred to her that faces were really something. You could know one so well with its familiar configurations of happy, ironic, and angry. The expressions so practiced, the lines drawn, waiting for emotions to fill out the final features. Then, out of the blue, comes a twitch of an eyebrow or a quarter turn of the mouth, and there it is, a combination never before seen: anguish, fear, and love.

Propping her elbows on her knees, Maggie rested her head in the hammock of her hands and breathed into her sleeves. "You won't have to. I've decided that enough is enough." Maggie reached into the pocket of her walking shorts and pulled out a green piece of paper. She unfolded it on the table and smoothed the creases with her hand. "This is my fix-my-life list. I worked on it last night while Martin was sleeping."

Julia looked from the note to Maggie. The earnest look on Maggie's face showed no self-consciousness or understanding of how silly the list looked. The fat-lettered *To Do* on the top of the page, the underlined emphasis, the exclamation points after crossed-off number two: *Be nice to Martin!!*

"Here, look at number five." Maggie was awkwardly trying to cover up number three—*Do not call Julia*—but Julia inched her finger out of the way. She looked into Maggie's eyes. Maggie shrugged and said, "Oh, shut up."

"Jesus Christ, Maggie, anything else? How about putting world peace on your list?" Maggie ignored her and concentrated on trying to smooth the lower half of the paper.

Julia said, "Okay, but I imagine forgetting everything about Craig Tyson/David is going to be difficult since I bet you want to know everything even more now."

"I trusted him." A car alarm went off in the distance, alerting the world to Maggie's honest declaration.

"So, how are you going to do it? Deal with not knowing, I mean."

With calm fortitude Maggie said, "I'm just going to walk away."

"Yeah?"

"Yeah. I'm going to focus on Martin, this baby, and getting ready for the next phase of my life. Good-bye, Neighborhood Watch. Hello, new mother. By the way, you didn't tell Martin that I'm obsessed with Tyson/David, did you?"

"I bet he guessed it when you were hunched over doing whatever it is you do there."

"No, I mean, you didn't tell him I thought . . . one of them, the David one, was cute, did you? Because the thought of it now really nauseates me."

"Christ, what do you take me for? I may be a meddler, but I'm a friendly meddler. I work for good, not evil."

## *Hand Over Hand Over Hand*

It was early evening when Maggie returned home from Julia's and the day was tossing all of the heavy ingredients of summer into the hopper. A recipe straight from the equator: creamy humidity, bubbled tar driveways, and Popsicle sticks floating in pools of blue syrup. Even the squirrels felt too full of summer soup to chatter. Maggie opened her storm door and released a pamphlet that lay curled in the handle. She read the title as it fluttered to her feet on the front stoop: *Is There a Creator Who Cares about You?* If the answer was no, she didn't want to know about it today.

It was softball night and Maggie had given Martin her blessing.

"Stay out and play honey. Have a drink after," she had said. "I'm going to bed right now."

"What should I do if Tyson shows up?"

Maggie had shrugged and said, "Call the police, come home, stay and play. I don't care one way or another."

Now she stood in the doorway, taking a moment to breathe in the familiar mixture of coffee, Mr. Clean, and cookies. Maggie rarely baked and almost never had cookies in the house, but the sweet smell of almond and butter floated in and around the floorboards like the spirit of bakers past. She gazed at her uncluttered living room and realized it had the feel of a furniture showroom. The colors were muted and tasteful, the artificial ficus tree perfectly and forever watered, never outgrowing its roots.

Charming pillows sat fat and happy on the couch right where she'd left them. Martin's cereal bowl was sure to be in the dishwasher, the counters wiped of crumbs. It looked sterile and uninviting, like a home where no real people lived. She walked to the couch, tossed the pillows on the floor and gave one a kick. *There*, she thought.

In the kitchen, she looked up at the ceiling fan, the friendliest of the home-lighting accessories, gently waving like the Tobacco Princess in the Memorial Day Parade. She hit the wall switch. When the fan slowed to a stop, Maggie stood on a chair, grabbed one of the paddles, and hung from it until it snapped. The base of the fan came partially loose from its moorings and a piece of the ceiling dropped onto the table.

She pressed her hands across her belly, feeling a tightening followed by a release. If the baby was moving, Maggie knew all would be well. She looked up and out her window when she heard muted laughter from her neighbors next door. The little girls who lived there pushed out of their house like bees were chasing them. The oldest one jogged full out, straight brown hair flying back from her face, legs athletic and sure. Her feet were bare and she moved as if the possibility of a sharp rock were as improbable as encountering a hippopotamus in the middle of Wisconsin. The smaller girl followed her big sister; she was hindered slightly by her light blue fluffy slippers. Her yellow tutu bounced and the purple feather boa around her neck dropped to the ground. She had a head of dark curls that flew in a tangle of indecision on her head, and she was shirtless.

Having reached the wooden play structure, the older girl climbed and started across the monkey bars. *Who said girls lacked upper-body strength?* thought Maggie. They certainly had it when they were young. It's too bad they don't realize that practicing on the bars is perfect training for life: hand over hand over hand.

The smaller girl was deep into a head-back/arms-out spin. She stopped, staggered, and fell, bumping her head on the yellow plastic slide. Maggie could hear her outrage loud and clear from where she sat in her kitchen, and she watched as the older girl dropped midreach and went to her. She brushed her sister's hair back to examine the injury and leaned forward to kiss it. The younger girl touched her sister's hair, letting the strands slide through her fingers.

The evening turned dark while Maggie sat. The shadows grew and disappeared. The play outside turned to bedtime stories inside. Maggie showered and dressed. Carefully, she placed two eggs from the refrigerator door inside the pocket of her large maternity smock, padding them with paper towels. Her arms shook slightly as she steered the bike down the driveway.

The summer heat dissipated as she coasted on her bike. Maggie arched her back, pressing one hand into her hip. She repositioned her belly. Though only nine thirty, it was an inky black night; the sky was filled with velvet clouds.

She had wanted to confront him, to say, "Hey, jackass, I can't believe you're a sex offender," to slap his face. But this last message, this last show of force, would have to be enough.

She braked to slow her progression. Her heart started

pumping blood like a line of volunteer firemen in a bucket brigade. Fill, throw, fill, throw. She wanted to reach into her chest and pat it down, shush it, hold its veiny hand.

She could see David's house up ahead. The outline of the shutters, the geraniums, a new sign—*No Solicitors*—hanging on the light post. Maggie slowed the bike, reached into her pocket, and grasped both eggs. With one hand steadying the handlebars and the other overhead, she let go with a pitch that Willie Mays would be proud of. She braked to enjoy the arc and majesty of her final good-bye and watched in horror as both eggs hit the grass, one landing in the center of the lawn like a pearly beacon and the other rolling under the hedge, intact.

Pedaling, panicked, she biked to the end of the block and turned the corner. Fingerprints. Maggie knew she had to go back. She had to get the eggs.

"Shit, shit, shit. How could you be so stupid?" she muttered to herself.

Making a large awkward arc, she headed back to the house. Ungracefully, she dropped the bike next to the large hedge at the edge of the property and stepped free of it. Standing at the edge of the driveway, she saw that all four tires were inflated on the car, but it sat guarded, closer to the house.

Maggie stopped to catch her breath. Feeling a little dizzy, she bent forward and put her head down. After a minute of rest, she walked to the center of the lawn. Swiping the unbroken egg from the grass, she noticed for the first time its heft and weight. Hard-boiled.

She glanced around quickly and listened. Straightening she put her hands on her hips and arched her back. *God, I'm uncomfortable tonight.*

Easing herself to the ground, she moved quickly to the spot where the egg had entered the hedge. On her hands and knees, she began to crawl a few inches under the bush, reaching in and forward. Branches struck her in the temple and she brushed them noisily aside and muttered, "I can't see a thing." Maggie pushed back on her haunches and tried to pull the branches apart to get a better view. Suddenly, a bright light lit up the area and she could see the egg, plain as day.

She retrieved it and slipped it into her pocket looking over her shoulders into the searchlight. She shielded her eyes with her arm and squinted. A male voice said, "All right, who's in there? Come on out. Slowly."

Maggie closed her eyes and felt the wet cement of dread seep into her abdomen. She crawled back and with an ungainly effort stood. The light blinded her.

She could hear the scuff of the policeman's shoes as he moved across the lawn to her. Looking askance he said, "Is that you, Mrs. Finley? What in the hell are you doing out here?"

The porch light went on. Maggie heard several clicks and the suction of air as the front door opened. The screen moved outward and a woman appeared with a look of concern on her face.

"Can I help you?"

Maggie lifted her head, straightened her shoulders, and tried to calm her nerves with a friendly smile. The woman wore a mango-colored shirt with the collar up over a white T-shirt and jeans. Her hair was short, mostly gray, and styled like old photos of Audrey Hepburn—short bangs, tight around her ears, and ready for anything. She was holding a telephone.

The officer straightened his cap, plucked at the collar of his uniform, and said, "Good evening, Eleanor. I spotted this woman on your lawn while checking out a disturbance call in the area."

Maggie spoke up. "I'm sorry. I was going to knock, but I felt a little dizzy. I needed a second." She turned sideways, the better to display her pregnancy. "I'm David's friend, Maggie."

The policeman said, "Okay, let's take a walk over to the car and you can tell me what's going on."

"Edward. No, it's fine. I didn't know Maggie was stopping by, but how nice." The woman took a few steps onto the front porch, letting the screen door slam behind her. "It's wonderful that you're keeping an eye on the neighborhood. I feel so safe." She smiled winningly, making Maggie think of her mother.

Unconvinced, Edward glared at Maggie. "Could this be the vandal you've been calling the station about?"

With a scathing look at the policeman Eleanor said, "Does she look like a common vandal? She's pregnant, for God's sake; she's got better things to do with her time than harass little old ladies."

Chastised, the patrolman straightened his pants. Maggie began to drift closer to the steps of the house.

"Look, ladies, we're busy, okay? I don't know what's going on here, but I'll let you two deal with it." Then to Maggie he said, "I thought the next time I saw you would be at your meeting. Remember when we talked about how to recognize suspicious activity? Well, you can put this on the top of that list." He pulled his shoulders back, bringing him up to his full height. "If you need me, El, you know where to find me."

"I do, Edward. Thank you."

Maggie exhaled, feeling the weight of the eggs in her pocket. The two women watched as the police car pulled away from the curb and Eleanor gave a friendly little wave.

"He's got a little case of the Ellie's, if you know what I mean. He's nice, but I like my space."

Maggie took a few steps toward the woman and reached for her hand. "We've never met, but David and I went to an auction together and sometimes he helps me around the house."

"He's very handy, my boy." The woman touched Maggie gently. Her fingertips were soft. "It's so nice to finally meet you. Don't you look lovely? Pregnancy becomes you. Some women never really take to it." She stepped back into the doorway as she said this and opened the screen wide. Maggie could see a brightened room with gauzy curtains that looked quiet and inviting. "When are you due? Last time I asked David, he couldn't remember. You know, I think it's beyond men's understanding, don't you?" Eleanor escorted Maggie inside.

"About two months," Maggie said, and then added, "Men don't seem to have much appreciation for the inner workings of women. No baseline, I guess."

"That's exactly it, isn't it? Well put. No baseline," she repeated. "I mean, it would be like trying to empathize with lightning bugs or hummingbirds. Wrong species."

"So, you're David's mother. He speaks of you often."

"Eleanor. My name is Eleanor. I never liked the name, but it's mine. I fancied myself a Judy or Jackie, but then so did everyone of my generation. Garland or Kennedy unless you wanted to go the Marilyn route, but I always thought that name a bit overt." Eleanor tucked a strand of hair behind her ear. "Now, Maggie, that's a good Irish name." Listening, Maggie watched her face. David had the same dimple and her unsung gray eyes. She must have been very pretty when she was younger.

"Yes, it is Irish. My father was full Irish and told me to never let anyone call me Margaret. He thought I was a Maggie through and through. He's dead now."

"Oh, I'm sorry for your loss." And then after a quiet moment said, "Loss is everywhere, isn't it? Life should be called loss. It should be a synonym that you look up in a dictionary. It would help people so much to understand this early on. We would make such different choices, don't you think?"

"Yes," said Maggie sincerely and then, remembering herself and where she was, said, "Is David here?"

"Oh, no. That's strange, didn't he tell you? I guess it was kind of last minute. He left today. He's gone to visit Susanne in France. She was taking some time off and they were going to do some traveling together. I imagine he's part of the way there by now. It was time for him to get on with his life. He moves around a lot. I don't know how he does it."

When Maggie was seven, she fell from a neighbor's tree house and landed on her chest. For a moment she lay in wonderment. Would she breathe again? Would she? Then the need for oxygen overcame her startled lungs, and she pulled air in like the sails on a ship. Today, Maggie tried hard to mask her feelings. She felt a slideshow of emotion play across her face and the combination of astonishment, disappointment, regret, and anger gripped her. A soft hand pulled her nearer to the living room. "Maybe you should sit, honey. You look a little disoriented. How about I get you some lemonade?"

Maggie tucked herself into the cool chintz of the sofa and waited for Eleanor to return. David had left without a word. Why was this fact bothering her? He was a sexual predator! What was wrong with her head? Still, what the heck was it with some men? Who leaves without saying good-bye? Maggie had only just met Eleanor and if Maggie got up from her seat and walked out the front door, she would call *good-bye* and even add a wave. Even her delinquent father said his good-byes. Granted, they were evasive and often more like *after a while, crocodile*, but still.

Maggie considered that maybe David's charge of secondary sexual assault was because of toying with someone's emotions and then disappearing. *No*, she thought, *I am not going to cry. Not here in his house in front of his mother.*

She felt a turning in her abdomen. *This baby must be on one hell of a roller-coaster ride*, thought Maggie as she smoothed her shirt over her belly and gave her trousers a yank. It had to be like surfing in there, tides turning on a dime. *Hang in there, honey*, she thought, *this is just the beginning. You might as well get used to it.*

Eleanor reappeared with two tall glasses of lemonade and handed one to Maggie. "Extra sugar because you look pale." There was an overstuffed chair to Maggie's right and Eleanor eased herself into it, watching Maggie under the microscope of her bifocals. "Are you sure David didn't mention he was leaving and you just forgot? When I was pregnant, I remember thinking I was losing my mind. Every time I had to give my phone number to someone I would forget it. Like the question itself was the eraser that wiped it from my mind."

When Maggie looked up through her drinking glass and saw Eleanor's concerned squint, she forced herself to compose the expression on her face. She swallowed and said, "No, I'm certain he never mentioned it. But it wasn't his job to keep me informed." She said this with a smile that tried to shrug away any hard feelings. Then it dawned on her that it was entirely possible David had left before she deflated the tire on the Honda, in which case this lovely woman would have been left with the carnage. Maggie cleared her throat and asked, "When did he leave?"

"Well, his ticket was for 7:55 this morning, but when we tried to leave for the airport, we had some trouble with the car." With a slight hesitation, she corrected herself and said, "The tires. One was flat as a pancake and had to be changed." Maggie could see a flex in Eleanor's temple as she clenched her jaw. "He missed his first flight and had to fly standby to make a connection in Chicago."

*Good*, Maggie thought, at least his escape had been delayed because of her. At least she had caused him some distress. Sipping and swallowing the sunny drink, she cleared her throat and said, "How long ago did you say he had planned this visit to see Susanne?"

"Let me think about that. Less than a week."

"Well," Maggie said, "it's not like he owed me his schedule or anything. We were new friends, after all."

"Yes, that's true," said Eleanor. "Still, he spoke of you and your husband with great fondness. It's not like David to be so impolite."

*Yes, exactly, thank you*, thought Maggie. She knew in a rush of emotions that she and Eleanor could have been great friends.

Eleanor looked up from her drink. The napkin she had wrapped at the base of her glass was wet with condensation and partially dissolved, the white paper no match for the stress of the day. "Is that why you're here, Maggie. To see David?"

"I . . . yes. I wanted to, ah, talk to him about . . ." Maggie put a hand to her forehead. "Boy. You are so right about that eraser. I can't seem to remember what I wanted."

Eleanor leveled her gaze and measured Maggie's face

with her eyes. She didn't speak for a moment, letting the crickets and frogs of the night take over the conversation. She took another sip from her glass and said, "I was so happy he found you and your husband to spend time with. He has a tendency to live privately and can be sort of unsociable. It was that way for years before he met Susanne, his fiancée. Then she moved, and the trouble started again. I worried he would just sort of fold up."

In a movie, there would be swelling music, an upsurge of strings, a moment when in spite of themselves, members of the audience would yell, *No, don't go in the basement alone! Don't do it!* As if she were watching herself from across the room, Maggie said, "Trouble?"

"You know the nuisance things of the last month. The damaged geraniums, the unwanted pizza deliveries, the pamphlets from religious fanatics."

"The bleach on the lawn," Maggie added.

"Oh," Eleanor said, narrowing her eyes, "is that what you think it was? David and I weren't sure, but it killed quite a patch in the front yard. We planted a tree there, sort of as a symbol. People can be so creatively treacherous."

"Yes, they certainly can," Maggie said. She thought of David's face at the coffee shop, pictured him walking out the door.

Maggie sat quietly next to Eleanor, who clearly was engaged in thoughts of her own. She touched Eleanor's arm and said, "It must have been hard on you, never knowing when you would wake up and find some new trouble. I'm so sorry."

Eleanor waved away her apology. "*Yes*, you never get used to it. You know, it was fairly predictable until recently. David knows that whenever he relocates, there's a rash of reactions until everyone gets the information they need. Then, after people hear his history and get to know him, the mischief goes away. This is the first time that it restarted more than a year after he moved in—and seemingly out of the blue."

Eleanor removed the sodden napkin from her now-empty glass and held it in her fist. She placed her glass on a coaster on the coffee table and breathed a soggy sigh. "Since this is his hometown, we had hopes it might be different. Plus, he moved home to take care of me. I thought that should count for something. I miss Dan, my husband." She gave a helpless shrug.

Maggie considered this woman in front of her and had a fleeting vision of her mother trying to explain her father's behavior to the neighbors. A sharp pain made her shift positions and she released a small puff of exertion.

Eleanor, mistaking Maggie's sigh for an urging to continue, said, "David thinks it was some kid who maybe went online and was just exercising his intimidation muscle. I wasn't sure about that. I kind of thought it was something more complicated. The abuse was subtle, almost gentle this time, not the kind of thing an angry teen might do. It's hard to figure. I don't blame them entirely. I mean, if the police notified me that my neighbor had a, shall we say, shady history, I wouldn't like it. I wouldn't attack them, but I probably wouldn't pursue a friendship either. It's hard to be objective anymore."

Maggie cringed. One of the nights she had been in front of this house something flew precariously close to Maggie's ear. She sensed it coming, felt the whisper of wings, and saw what looked like smoke veer away. This conversation was the figurative equivalent to that night, that feeling. Quickly she said, "Eleanor, can I ask you a question?"

Eleanor squared her shoulders and leaned toward Maggie. "Of course you can. It's nice to talk about this with someone other than David. He's so protective of me. I never like delving too far into motivations and theories."

Maggie went on. "I know about the vandalism, but what I don't know is why? What exactly are you talking about? He didn't talk about his past; *we* didn't talk about that. I think he tried once to tell me but was interrupted."

"I'm so sorry. I just assumed he told you. Maybe he was sick of starting friendships behind the eight ball and decided not to risk it with you. I suppose it makes sense that you wouldn't know." Eleanor cleared her throat and looked at her hands. She picked at a piece of cuticle and rubbed her knuckles.

"David was born in Michigan, in our kitchen! His birthday is coming up in September. He was such a smart boy, reading in preschool and writing stories. He was so ready for kindergarten, excited to be a big boy. I remember his sweet face telling me how he would help the others read because he wanted to be a teacher when he grew up. A teacher/lion tamer, of course." Eleanor stopped speaking as she sat with her memory, an old friend with a supportive shoulder. "My husband and I had to decide if we would send him early to kindergarten or hang on to him because of his late birthday. Dan was a slight man, always the last picked for sport teams, and didn't want David to be in the same boat. He thought it might be best to hang on to him and let him be the biggest and smartest. You always want the best for your children. You'll see."

Maggie watched as Eleanor opened cabinets of the past, as she pulled out memories and fluffed them, inspected them for lapses, clarity. For a moment, Maggie saw David's dark-haired self, smiling, holding a paper-bag lunch and a number two pencil. She reached out for Eleanor and said, "No, Eleanor, stop. You don't have to tell me. You don't have to revisit this. I am being purely selfish."

But Eleanor did not see the miles of truth in this statement. She looked again at Maggie and said, "I don't mind . . . I want to. It's good to remember the past and see how far the journey has come since then." Eleanor looked up at a spot on the ceiling as if part of the memory lived in the rafters. "He grew so tall, and, well, you know how handsome." She smiled like only a mother can, remembering her now-grown son's every freckle. "It was nice for him to be the oldest, the best at sports and school, the first to drive. He was softhearted, too. The girls called all the time." Eleanor gave a kind of pained smile at the memory, swallowed, and went on. "When he was a senior, almost ready to graduate, he got mixed up with one of them. Cheri. She spelled it the French way and all. He met her in an art class. Dan and I joked about her and called her the 'art tart.' She was trouble and I knew it the minute she parked her petite feet on our stoop. She had this extremely sexy way about her, you know how some are. She even made Dan feel funny. David didn't have a chance. Where does a fifteen-year-old girl learn such things? I'll never know."

Maggie heard the same air-conditioning unit from the other night kick on, and in her mind saw Eleanor, her makeup off, sleeping in her bed under the lace curtains. She saw the anxiety gone around her eyes, her wedding rings loose on her left ring finger. Maggie's breath caught again and she swallowed a fat lump of feeling—shame? fear?—that was looking for permission to tumble out.

"It's a short story from here on out. This girl's father and mother were at a local restaurant and David went to watch a movie at Cheri's house. He was eighteen and she was fifteen. This was like fertilizer for a felony. Her parents came home early, walked in on them, and that was the end of David's life as we knew it. Statutory rape. The girl claimed she was coerced, and with the way the law was written and their ages, it was his word against hers. Anyway, we made a deal and forever after my son's sweet face will be recorded online as if he's some kind of predatory animal. *Coerced*, my rear end. The girl just sat back and watched it unfold."

Eleanor rubbed her eyes and said, "It just frosts me that delaying kindergarten thirteen years before sealed his fate. The moral of that story? Everything has a consequence. Winter is the bill for a long, sunny summer."

Blood roared in Maggie's ears. Was she going to vomit now? This new information and the summer heat joined the sour lemon syrup at her epiglottis for a momentary conference. She lurched forward and gagged, reaching for Eleanor's innocent potpourri dish.

Eleanor jumped. "Lord! Oh my, Maggie. I'll get a rag." She nearly ran to the kitchen. Maggie dry heaved once, twice, and a third time for emphasis alone. Her esophagus was so unbelievably fed up with having to swallow her enormous emotional pie, each bite too big for any normal-sized organ. *For Christ's sake*, it seemed to say.

When Eleanor returned with a towel, she handed it to Maggie and said, "I'm so sorry, going on like that. Don't worry for a minute about this, Maggie. I always had terrible nausea when I was pregnant. You never get a warning when the bile rises, do you?"

Maggie stood. "I really don't feel good." As she met Eleanor's clear gray eyes, she felt a warm gush of water followed by a seizing deep within her. She staggered, resting her weight on the arm of the chair and said, "God, I think, my water broke."

Eleanor's face brightened with expectation, saying, "Oh my!" She placed her hand on Maggie's shoulder and said, "Sit back down, sweetie. Don't worry about the couch. This is wonderful."

"No!" Maggie cried sharply. "You don't understand. I'm only thirty-six weeks. It's too early."

Eleanor looked into Maggie's contorted face. She registered her fear, saw her red face go pale. Wanting to reassure her, she said, "This isn't that unusual. We'll get you to the hospital in time."

Maggie grabbed Eleanor's arm and squeezed. She was frantic now. "They were going to induce me. I shouldn't be doing this. This is wrong!" She let go of Eleanor and covered her face with her hands. "This isn't happening."

"All right then. Try to relax and let's get you to the car. Lean on me, I'm stronger than I look."

Eleanor set her jaw and reached around Maggie's back. Maggie had both arms cradling her belly. She could feel the wet thin cotton of her shirt, cool and clammy against her skin. She pictured her sweat evaporating and taking her child with it.

Moving toward the door with Eleanor she nearly shouted, "I've got to call Martin." Then she began to cry. "I need my husband. I need him here."

Eleanor grabbed her purse, which hung from the doorknob by its strap. Yanking the door open, she eased Maggie through the opening and together they shuffled down the entry stairs.

"Call him in the car. No need for tears just yet, honey."

"You don't understand. My first baby died! Ella, my first. She died in my belly."

Just as she helped Maggie into the car, Eleanor said with an intensity built on years of understanding pain, with the certainty of experience, "This is not your first. This is your *second.* And she's going to be fine."

Eleanor jogged around and wrenched open the driver's side door. She sat and started the car and glanced at Maggie. Maggie was staring at her belly, still with her arms wrapped around her large, round girth. "I feel like I'm expanding like a balloon. My back is killing me. There's still water coming out!"

With calm authority Eleanor said, "Concentrate on calling your husband." The green Honda with the newly inflated tire left a black smear of rubber in the driveway as Eleanor gunned the accelerator.

Maggie dialed. Into her phone she shouted, "Martin, can't you ever pick up your goddamned phone? My water broke. Meet me at the hospital."

Eleanor barked at Maggie, "Start counting those contractions. And fasten your seatbelt."

# *Say Hello*

Maggie's eyes darted around the newly renovated labor and delivery room. Martin was standing by the door deep in conversation with a man in scrubs. The walls were painted peachy beige and smoky blue in an attempt to make the place appear homey and calm, but it wasn't working for her. The nurse at Maggie's shoulder was threading clear IV tubing through the sleeve of her hospital gown. An unknown woman standing between her legs spoke in a soothing tone.

"Relax a little, let your knees fall to the side. Just checking for dilation." A man was squirting cold gel on her belly.

"How are you feeling, Maggie?" Maggie looked into the ice blue eyes of the woman at her shoulder. She had placed her cool hand in the spot where Maggie's neck and shoulder met. "My back is killing me and this room is hot as hell." A fat tear rolled out of the corner of her eye and Maggie let it drop onto the nurse's hand.

"I'm scared." She croaked out a flimsy, "Martin?"

Maggie braced her arms at her sides and the tendons of her neck stood out.

The woman with the cold hands moved so her head blocked the view of the room. "You look scared to death," she said. "Listen to me. You don't need to be afraid right now. Look around you. Everything is going well. The baby's heart is strong. That strap around your middle is going to tell us how the baby is tracking."

"But my first child . . ." Maggie began, but the nurse interrupted her.

"I know all about her, but this is the baby that needs you now. And she's getting ready to meet her mother."

Maggie started to cry in earnest but a contraction cut her off and she inhaled sharply. She closed her eyes.

When she opened them, Martin was standing by her side with a plastic glass of ice chips and a gray expression of terror.

"We're not supposed to be afraid," said Maggie reaching for the glass of ice.

"I'm not afraid for you. I know you can do this. I'm afraid for me. I feel like I'm going to throw up."

"Don't you dare, Martin. So help me."

He put his hand on her belly. "Does it feel like last time?" She smelled the mustiness of that day, the rain. The traffic noise crowded in on her. She remembered the silence from the heart-rate monitor. The emptiness in the faces of the doctors and nurses.

She saw her father's face from when she was a child. *Maggie,* he used to say, *Maggie, you are a pistol, that's for sure.* She pushed herself up and repositioned into an almost seated posture.

"It's worse, I think."

"They want to know if you want an epidural."

The beginning of a low, dark heat began under her navel and traveled like a web across her belly. She squeezed her eyes shut and tried to breathe through pursed lips. She visualized climbing up and out of a well of black. She felt a bead of sweat run down from her temple. When the darkness turned to light and scrambled away, she opened her eyes and said, "No way, I don't want to miss a single ache, or rob this body of one ounce of glory."

"You don't have to be a hero, Mags. I'd take the drugs."

"I will for the next one."

"You're the boss," said Martin, nodding.

* * *

After an hour, a very tall, blond man—looking more high school basketball star than medical professional—walked into the room, said a few words to the nurse, and shook Martin's hand. "I'm Lance Wheeler," he said to Maggie. "I'm the intern for Dr. Ng. He said he'll be right over and that I should check your cervix. See how you're doing."

Maggie eyed his hands and said, just before closing her eyes for another contraction, "No way. Hands too big. Get Ng."

"No need for any of that," said the nurse standing between Maggie's bent knees. "The baby's crowning." The activity in the room sped into a crazy fast-forwarded movie. Her body was positioned. Martin was placed at Maggie's shoulder and the bed became a tilt-a-whirl of swinging handles and paddles. No longer on her back, she could now see the room in full. Dr. Ng seemed to appear out of nowhere and this struck Maggie as funny, so she smiled and said to the nurse, "Men only ever have to show up."

The nurse nodded and said, "Okay, Maggie. This is your show. It's all you and this baby. Forget everything and push."

The red haze that came over Maggie as she grasped the handles of her bed came from a place that only she knew existed. She made no sound, wasted no energy, and visualized the sunny ray of love she always felt when thinking of her child as she pushed the baby into the world.

Dr. Ng said, "Beautiful. She's beautiful."

Maggie hesitated for just a second then looked at Martin, whose face was blotchy, wet, and filled with tenderness. He nodded. Maggie sat back and watched while hands grasped her child, clearing eyes and airways. The pale arms of the medical team were in sharp contrast to the slippery, red-skinned child. The baby's face was full, florid, and filled with rage as she sang out her first admonishment.

Maggie said to no one and everyone, "I did it. She's here. She's okay." She was vaguely aware of something happening between her legs and marveled at how little she cared.

Dr. Ng said, "I hope you won't be disappointed, Martin, but nobody cuts the cord but me. I've found giving a highly emotional, dizzy father a sharp object near tender tissue is never a good idea."

Martin wiped his face and said, "No sweat, I've got better things to do up here." And he leaned forward to kiss Maggie and say hello to his daughter.

# *It Was You*

"Five pounds, one ounce. That's a respectable size for a preemie." Maggie's mother sat holding the baby in the chair next to the hospital bed. "You were only six and a half pounds, and I carried you all the way till the fat lady sang." Shaking her head warmly while gazing at the onion skin that doubled as infant eyelids, she added, "You were mulish even then." Maggie smiled at her mother, who was snuggling her daughter. She felt for all the world like the patron saint of completion and beneficence.

"I did it, Mom."

Her mother stood, carefully holding her light-as-a-feather granddaughter, and sat on the edge of the bed.

"Of course you did, sweetie. I never had even a moment of doubt. Of course you did."

She placed the baby into Maggie's arms. "You better take her. She's trying to nurse her fist. Then it's time for some sunshine. We have to get rid of that amber glow of hers."

Maggie placed the baby to her breast and sighed, "I imagine this will hurt when I'm off the pain meds."

"A little, but in a good way. Where are that husband and best friend of yours? I feel like hugging some people."

"They're getting me something to eat. I'm absolutely starving."

Reaching into a large canvas bag on the floor, Maggie's mother pulled out a small vinyl lunch bag. "Your favorite sandwich still lettuce, salt, and mayonnaise?"

"You didn't?" Maggie thinned her lips into a tiny ironic grin. "You're not the make-food-as-comfort kind of mom, Mom."

"Maybe if I had been, you would have always known you could do this. You'd have had fewer doubts about yourself."

Her mother opened the bag and took out the sandwich she had made.

With her free hand, Maggie took her childhood favorite and said, "I always hated bologna."

"Which is why I never had to worry about the mortgage. I paid it with bologna money."

"Remember how you used to let me bike around in your wedding dress?"

"Yeah, that was a mistake." Her mother rolled her eyes to the ceiling and added, "I made a lot of them. I thought that if I denied the mammoth-ness of marriage, I might be able to cope with a husband that I couldn't keep home." She reached out and cupped Maggie's chin.

Maggie loved her mother's hands. All these years later they still always smelled of lemons. The softness of those hands felt like what she imagined love would feel like if you took a butter knife and spread it on your face. They looked at each other, and her mother said, "Are you too old to play cuddle fish?"

On vacation, when Maggie was six, before the trouble started, Maggie, her father, and her mother had wandered through a fish market, reading the names of the fish and picking up scattered iridescent scales. She held the hands of both her parents and they laughed together at the ugly, bulbous fish eyes, pale underbellies, and ridiculous stunted side fins. Dolphin, tuna, kitty-catfish, and monkfish. "Bless me, fishy, for I have sinned," her father had joked.

A short way off by themselves, packed tightly together, were the cuttlefish. When Maggie's father saw them, he lifted Maggie and pressed her to him. She tucked her face against his five o'clock shadow. The smell of sandalwood and the warmth of his body made her feel like a kitten grabbed by the scruff of the neck, paralyzed but happy. Her mother had come up from behind and hugged them. She pressed her lips to Maggie's neck and whispered, "*Cuddle* fish." And then they all said it together just loud enough for each other to hear.

Now, her mother turned so she sat resting on the elevated head of the hospital bed. Maggie leaned her back into her mother's chest. The three generations sat and Maggie snuggled in as her own daughter moved into her.

Maggie sighed and said, "Remember the night the police came?"

"How could I forget?"

"I thought they came because you ran that red light earlier in the day. I slid off the backseat when you hit the brakes."

"I remember the thud you made."

"It's the first time I heard you swear. You said, 'Crap, I hope that policeman is more interested in his coffee than my driving.' You told me to look straight ahead and act *i-n-n-o-c-e-n-t*."

"I was a piece of work back then."

"You still are."

"How does that saying go? The nut doesn't fall far from the squirrel."

"I was worried that they'd come to our house to throw

you in jail. It never occurred to me they were there to tell us about Daddy."

"Why would you? It had been a long time since we'd last seen him."

Maggie sighed. "I'll never forget that guy's words. 'He was twenty miles away. If it wasn't for the rain and the flooded culvert, he would have made it just fine.' Like it was still a possibility."

"Do you still have the stuffed mouse the policeman found at the scene, the one Daddy bought for you?"

"Yeah, I do."

"When he handed me that leather manicure set with my initials embossed next to the zipper, I realized how long it had been since we had been a family."

"I was too old for stuffed animals."

"And my nails were chewed to the nub."

"Mom? Why did you stay with Dad?"

Her mother pulled away from Maggie and moved over on the hospital bed so that they could face each other. "I stayed . . . I stayed because he needed to be able to come home to you. It's what kept him alive. You were the reason he kept coming back, even though his alcoholism fought him at every turn. It was you, honey, it was always you."

There are days, Maggie knew, days and weeks and months that go by without event. The sun rises, newspapers are delivered, and not a single fault line is disturbed.

Then there are the other times when the information gods hit one out of the park and data floods in unchecked. Chewing her sandwich, Maggie swallowed salty mayonnaise, fortified wheat bread, and the idea that her father had loved her. That it was love that had kept him coming and going.

People show affection in mysterious ways. Some make sandwiches, some come and go in a fog of alcohol, and still others damage property in the dark of night. She and her father: two peas in a pod. Dysfunctional displays of disguised affection were their genetic link.

"Wow."

"Yeah, wow. How could I have not told you that before? What must you have thought all these years?"

Maggie shrugged a little. "Y'know that cat we had that threw up every day of its nauseous life? I used to wake up in the night and hear her gagging. Sometimes I would step in her vomit going to the bathroom in the middle of the night. When I wanted to get rid of her, do you remember what you said?"

"God no, I barely even remember that cat."

"You said you don't get rid of family members just because they require a bit of work. You can't cash out and cut your losses when inconvenience strikes. What would the world come to? You just clean up the mess and move forward to the next one."

"I never knew when to quit, just like you. Maybe we can both work on loosening our grip a little, traveling a little more lightly through life."

"I guess I have to figure that out."

"Thank God for Martin. He isn't a movie star or sports hero. He's more like a good support bra than a pair of flashy implants. See, this is where you were smarter than I was . . . am. He's not an alcoholic, and he wouldn't leave you if you shaved your head and started speaking in tongues. Unlike your father, Martin never met a revolving door he didn't bang his head on."

"Speak of the devil."

Martin walked over to the bed, with Julia in tow. He held a tray of coffee and an assortment of what must have been every kind of sandwich and muffin they had on display at the cafeteria. Julia rushed just ahead of him with two enormous Mylar balloons in the shapes of a sun and a strawberry.

"I couldn't help myself. If I didn't make some kind of grand gesture I think I would have burst with unexpressed emotion."

"Nothing goes unexpressed with you, Julia. You don't have to underline it with inflatables."

"Just shut up and hand her over, you baby hog."

"She's my baby. I can hog her if I want to."

Maggie's mother disengaged herself and said, "I'm not

getting in the middle of this. C'mon, Martin, let's see what you have on that tray."

Julia stood over the bed and peeked at the new baby. Her lips were cherry red ribbons and a fray of dark hair snuck out from under a striped yellow stocking cap. "Martin tells me you're naming her Caitlyn after your mother."

"Look at her. Doesn't she look like a Caitlyn?"

"She does. Through and through."

"Thanks for coming, Julia. I know I haven't been very easy lately." Seeing the embarrassment in her friend's face, she added, "I was so glad it was you helping me in the shower before, instead of that student nurse. She'd take one look at this nude, baggy body and swear off sex forever."

"Maybe you should make a movie and send it around to local high schools. You could call it *Abstinence? No problem!*"

After a moment of quiet, Maggie said, "He's not a sex offender, you know. I mean, not a real one."

"I know. I met Eleanor downstairs. She was incredibly sweet and concerned. She told me what you were talking about when you went into labor."

"Oh, my gosh. You talked to her?"

"Well, yeah. We all did. Martin, your mom, and I."

Maggie closed her eyes and breathed a soft sigh. The

baby gurgled and started to wake but settled herself and quieted.

Opening her eyes, she said, "It was all fake fear, Julia. Just like this," and she gestured to her baby. "Maybe fake fear is what you make when there isn't anything else to do."

"Maybe fear helps you know you're being courageous. Having a baby after losing Ella takes courage." Julia smoothed Maggie's bangs away from her face and said, "It's not like you're not entitled to a little fear, Maggie." She held her friend's hand, tilted her head, and grinned. "Not today, though. Today you are permitted only unmitigated elation and truly acceptable joy. Today is a hootenanny."

## *Blue Sky and God*

Julia sat on the front step of Maggie's home, a newspaper open beside her. She stood and with a huge smile said, "Welcome home." Martin unhooked the infant seat as Maggie swung her legs out of the car. She reached around and grabbed the clear plastic seat and hooked her arm through it. Julia smirked. "Ah, the donut of episiotomy and hemorrhoidal shame. I am well acquainted with the donut. For a long time I spent more time with the donut than I did with my husband." Then she bent to whisper in Maggie's ear. "The donut understood me."

Martin waved at Julia. "Thanks for coming to help. Let's get them inside, then I have to run to the store for smaller diapers." He ducked his head inside the car and popped up looking around in indecision. He put the baby, strapped into her infant seat, on the curb and jogged to the house. Then, turning abruptly, he ran back to get the baby.

Julia took the keys from Maggie and shook her head. "Men." She unlocked the front door. Together they stepped into the cool, dark foyer. It took a few moments for Julia's eyes to adjust. As the room came into focus, she noticed the broken ceiling fan and raised her eyebrows at Maggie. Maggie stood in the living room, right next to the pillow that sat abandoned and lonely on the floor. It seemed to look at her and say, *What'd I do?* She placed the pillow back on the couch.

Martin came in and gently placed the baby, in her car seat, on the floor in the kitchen. Without speaking, he spun around and raced out the door. The women followed him with their eyes, feeling the fluff of air as the door slammed shut. A moment later Martin poked his head back inside. "I'll be right back. I love you."

"Big Steven was a spaz, too. He'll calm down." Julia moved to pour a glass of water as Maggie sank with a loose heaviness into a kitchen chair.

"I don't really blame him," Maggie said. "There's a lot we don't have. Never for a moment did I think Caitlyn would come early. I guess I was a bit preoccupied."

Julia sat down across from Maggie and said, "Okay, lay it on me. Tell me what happened."

With broad, guilty strokes Maggie relayed the conversation she had the morning before she went into labor, painting a picture of Eleanor and David with Maggie the Devil lurking in the shadows.

"He was a kid! Just a kid. A horny, normal, eighteen-year-old kid who had hooked up with a shitty human being. No wonder he doesn't trust anyone. No wonder he doesn't use his real name." Then with renewed disgust, she whispered, "I chased him away. *I* did. I'm the only predator in this postage-stamp town. *I* am the Hemlock Street Stalker."

Julia let the self-flagellation go on until Maggie ran out of words. Then, she took a paper napkin from the center of the table and wiped Maggie's face with it.

"Okay, I get it," said Julia. "You suck." Maggie's face stiffened and Julia went on. "Yes, you got it wrong, and I hate to say I told you so but, shit, I told you so." Julia closed her eyes for a moment. "Still, here's the thing. It's done and I am not going to let you trash your whole existence because you were afraid, and also, maybe, a little bit in love. The most powerful and brilliant men and women of the ages have been bested by these twin sister emotions. What makes you so special that you should be immune?" Maggie blinked and wiped her nose on the back of her hand. The refrigerator hummed and Maggie's stomach growled, not ready to give up the fight.

"What am I going to tell Martin? He'll never understand when he hears all of it, what I've done. He's too sane for this kind of Shakespeare," Maggie said, looking like the dam was about to break.

Julia gave a wry smirk and said, "Not too sane. He married you, didn't he? If *he* doesn't understand fear and love, then I don't know who does."

Maggie exhaled, sending a clean napkin skittering across the table like a stingray.

Julia placed her hand on Maggie's wrist. "When Little Steven had meningitis I stopped eating," she said. "Not like a hunger strike or anything, it just felt like too much of a disloyalty. He was so sick. I was convinced he'd gotten it when I forced him to go to his swimming lessons. I thought I had fatally wounded my little boy because I wanted to get my money's worth."

Maggie blinked but didn't speak.

"I thought, how can I do something as selfish as take in food, enjoy it, and swallow when my child lay sick? I tried to explain it to Big Steven, but he didn't understand. Turns out he didn't really need to. But it sure gave him something to do. He's a fixer." Julia smiled warmly at the memory. "Every day he would come to the hospital with my favorite foods: ice cream, mashed potatoes and gravy, macaroni and cheese, and he would sit next to me and spoon it into my mouth. When I gagged, he would wait and then start again while chatting about the news or something that happened at work."

Maggie looked up at Julia's face. For the first time, she noticed a chicken pox scar on Julia's temple right next to a beige freckle. "It wasn't what I wanted, Mags. I wanted him to sit quietly next to me while I cried. I wanted him to rage at the doctors, demand a cure. I wanted him to curse like a rapper. But in the words of the famous philosopher M. Jagger, 'You can't always get what you want.' Give Martin a chance, honey. Give Martin a chance to figure out what you need."

There was a tentative tap at the door and Maggie groaned. "Tell whoever it is to go away, I can't face anyone right now," and she dropped her head to the table and placed her hands on her head. Julia's tennis shoes made a shuffling sound as she crossed the room. The sound of the front door opening made Maggie cringe inside.

"It's Big Steven. I'm outta here. You and Martin need some alone time and I've got my own bombshell to deliver."

Julia stepped outside and into the waiting car.

"How is she?"

"Let's go for a drive. I need a change of scenery."

"Where to, doll? You called for a driver and I'm here to do your bidding."

"I want to go to Razzelberry Highway Farm, that pick-your-own dynamo in the middle of blue sky and God." Big Steven accelerated and drove on. Julia inhaled deeply and settled back into her seat. As they approached the edge of town, they passed one of the town's original homesteads. The last and final holdout not taken over by the Creeping Charlie of urban sprawl. Julia remarked, "Is there anything more beautiful than a Wisconsin farm? So solitary and hopeful. The perfect red barn and a baby-bottle silo, with the four-square house standing nearby, proud and parental. A cow or two grazing, so spick-and-span." She turned her head as they passed the property. "They're more like props in the play of Wisconsin than a real, functional, dirty farm with ledger sheets and a fear of hail."

"Yep." Big Steven smiled a quiet smile. The farmland grew between them and Julia settled back in her seat. Gazing out the window she said, "I bought an amazing dress last week. It's a skin-tight wrap dress with a low V-neck and cap sleeves. A poster in the dressing room talked me into it. It was a photograph of Jamaica. There was a beautiful black man with eyes the color of the water and teeth as white and straight as mah-jongg tiles." She sighed. "He was holding dreadlocks away from his face and leering at me as if to say, 'Come to Jamaica, pretty lady, and bring the dress.' So I stripped to the strains of 'Dude (Looks Like a Lady),' in muted, piped-in dressing room Muzak, and tried it on, and bought it."

"When do I get to see you in this dress?"

"What would you say if I told you, in about ten months to a year, depending on weight gain and gravity?"

Big Steven dropped his foot from the accelerator and the car slowed. He brought it to a stop on the shoulder of the road, then turned his head and laughed. "Ha, I knew it. You give off your own scent when you're pregnant. Yes," he shouted and pumped his fist in the air. Julia had her sarcastic half smile on her face and waited for Big Steven to notice. He reached and grabbed her hand. "How do you feel about this?"

"Gee, thanks for asking. Are you done doing your fertility-touchdown dance?" She shook her head from side to side. "I wasn't feeling so great a few days ago."

"Better now?"

Julia shrugged. "Watching Maggie always struggle for the brass ring of a life is both frustrating and heartbreaking. Especially when she's pregnant and has such a good husband. It's just like her not to see the man for the freaks around her. Damaged goods everywhere, and the one shining example of future happiness is living under the same roof, and where is Maggie? Out cavorting with a group of people more interested in discord than harmony." She cleared her throat. "You know what Little Stevie said the other day? We were reading about Doctor Dolittle's Pushmi-pullyu pet. He said how weird it would be to have a pet who couldn't decide which way to go." Julia laced her fingers into her husband's hands and said, "I guess I was doing the same thing, only focusing on Maggie instead."

Big Steven frowned slightly but didn't speak.

"Lately I've felt like I'm in a holding pattern. As if I should be doing more for the world: saving Darfur, coming up with a solution for all the trash we're generating, or finding a fresh water supply for Africa. Like once I had some free time I could make a positive impact in the world. Like I did when I was a nurse. Then I realized that getting Michael to understand that playing with his penis in public isn't socially acceptable *is* a contribution to society."

Big Steven laughed. "I've barely learned that myself."

"You *haven't* learned that yourself. If your mother had worked a little harder on you, I might have time to learn French instead of constantly picking up your socks and making sure you don't have your hands in your pants."

Big Steven gave Julia a look of mock outrage and said, "Or your pants."

"So, this is what I'm doing now. I can save Darfur when the boys graduate from high school, but right now, Little Steven still wets the bed occasionally. I've got work to do here. Meaningful work."

Big Steven winked.

"Don't wink at me like you knew what was going on all along." Julia disengaged her hand from his and slugged him in the shoulder. "Are you ready for my body to throw a hormone party because every single bloated cell is invited? Are you ready for my very reasonable 36C breasts to become an aching 42DD overnight? Remember, these babies"—Julia indicated her chest—"are like plastic-covered living room couches. All the cushioning without any of the enjoyment. Untouchable by human hands. Reserved table for one, namely the curled bundle hiding deep inside of me."

"I'm ready."

"There's going to be nausea, tofu sausage fingers, and that weird mask of pregnancy that I always get on the left side of my chin. And as soon as I find out that this child is a girl, I am going to buy every gingham, rickrack-trimmed dress and onesie with cherries on it that I can find." As if to herself, she said, "God, I love red gingham.

If I had a barn, I would cover it with gingham and let the neighbors be damned."

Big Steven reached over and smoothed Julia's hair away from her face. "I love you," he said.

Julia narrowed her eyes. "Not for nothin'," she said, "we're getting a cleaning woman."

# *Talk of the Town*

"I don't think this is a good idea, Martin. I want to be done with this whole thing." Maggie was seated next to her husband, twirling her wedding ring and playing with the electric door lock in their van. "I've never seen Beverly Finker and I'd just as soon keep it that way."

"She's a pushy, nosy bully. You need to be clear that you're finished with the Neighborhood Watch and with her. She *has* to stop calling us and she won't stop as long as she has the upper hand. She obviously knows what you were doing at David's. We need to show her that you and I and Caitlyn are a unified front, that we have no secrets."

Maggie turned to check on their daughter sleeping

soundly in the backseat. The baby mirror pinned to the backseat confirmed that she was safe. "I'm a pushy, nosy bully, too, don't forget."

"Yes, you are, but you're *my* pushy, nosy bully, and I'm not sharing you with Beverly." Martin reached over and squeezed Maggie's thigh.

"My point is, it's going to sound pretty hollow when I tell her to mind her own business. How much weight will that carry coming from me?"

Martin pulled over to the side of the road and turned as far as his shoulder restraint allowed. "Get this straight. We are not doing this for her. We are doing this for you. You need closure and this is one step toward putting this behind us. She can go on to be the national president of all Neighborhood Watches everywhere for all I care. This is going to help you, and you are all I care about."

Maggie's eyes filled with tears and she choked out, "I'm sorry. I'm so sorry to have put you through this whole thing."

When she had finally told Martin the extent of her vandalism—what he called her "while-collar college-boy mischief"—she had felt incredible liberation. With the mostly empty surveillance folder, ball cap, sunglasses, and list of what amounted to silly pranks spread out in front of them, Maggie could see the futility and ridiculousness of her behavior.

On the other hand, she and Julia, in a different but related conversation, had decided there would be no confession of her attraction to David.

"You know that I am unbelievably hot for Little Steven's mini-ball soccer coach, right?" Julia was looking at Maggie with the piercing look of a very serious woman. "And you know that I stay after practice to help tear down the collapsible goals and retrieve balls just so I can watch him bend over." Maggie nodded, having known this for some time. "You are also aware that Big Steven will never, ever know this about me, and I will never know of his longtime obsession with the girl who serves frozen custard at Eggs 'n' Ice, right?

"Does Big Steven have an obsession with a girl at Eggs 'n' Ice?"

"I don't know. But if he did, I wouldn't want to know about it. Everyone has crushes. That's why they're crushes and not affairs. Mental crushes spice up your sex life; physical affairs spoil everything."

With Maggie's curious and confusing interest in David aside, all that was left to deal with was a pile of juvenile behavior and guilt. Maggie glanced at Martin and then out the front windshield.

"Once we cop to the vandalism, do you think she'll call the police?"

"Cop?"

Smiling a teary smile Maggie said, "Wait until I call myself the 'perp,' then we'll really get started."

"She won't call the police. She likes being the only one with information. We're going to own up to it and take the power out of that knowledge."

Martin pulled into the street and drove to Wilmington Way. Beverly's home was identical in size to Maggie's childhood home and had a world-class collection of wind chimes hanging from every corner and spike in the yard.

"Guess wind is her thing," said Maggie looking at Martin and stepping out of the van. "Better keep the engine running. I don't want Caitlyn to wake."

As they moved together onto the porch, the front door swung open and a woman came into view. She was the shape of a pencil eraser, square and stout. She pushed her hip into the door and leaned on a three-pronged aluminum cane. She was older than Maggie had expected. There wasn't much to distinguish her from a thousand other elderly women except that she wore a jet-black wig that covered the top half of her exceedingly white hair. *Andy Warhol in a square housedress*, Maggie thought.

"Maggie, dear, nice of you to visit, finally." The sneer that punctuated her greeting was only halfheartedly concealed as Beverly Finker sized up Martin and Maggie. "Don't you look just like your father? Course, I hardly remember him. Wasn't around much, as I recall." Beverly let the meanness of this statement sink in and then finished with another jewel. "It's your mother I remember."

"My mother?"

"You may look like your father but you have your mother's nature. What did the townies call her? Proud? It was never that, though, was it, Maggie? She was stuck up. Too good to accept any help, just like her daughter. Lord knows I tried to help every time I saw your father high-tailing it out of town."

Martin took a breath to speak and Maggie grabbed his forearm.

"You knew my parents?" A gust of air lifted Maggie's bangs as she waited for an outsider's view on her messy life.

"Didn't everybody? They were the talk of the town. Denny and I used to take bets on how long he'd hang around and what would happen to you." Without moving her head, her eyes darted to Martin. "So, this is your husband? Doesn't look anything like that drunk of a father of yours."

"All right, that's enough." Martin moved forward and placed his arm around Maggie.

"No, Martin, let her speak. She clearly has something to say to me and has been waiting a lot of years to say it."

"It's interesting, don't you think? Even with this good man at home, you are your mother's daughter—ultimately hanging around with trash. Don't think for a minute this town didn't see you riding around with that Tyson boy. Even in high school he wasn't satisfied with the nice girls. He wouldn't go out with my Bridget. Had to have the class slut." Beverly's eyes darted between Martin and Maggie as if she were gauging just how far she could go. "He got what he deserved, though, didn't he? I made that phone call all those years ago. I called the restaurant. I told that girl's parents to get home where they belonged." Beverly frowned. She looked a bit like a frog. "I didn't have to do much else but write a few letters to the newspaper after that."

Maggie recalled Eleanor explaining the night David was discovered with Cheri. She recalled the sadness in her voice. She recalled the unnamed emotion on David's face in his online mug shot, the emotion she could finally put a label on: innocence lost. But Beverly wasn't finished.

"When he moved back home recently, I thought I had my work cut out for me, but you saved me some trouble there, and I thank you for that. I couldn't figure why you were friendly to him one minute and harassing him the next, but 'ours not to reason why, ours but to do and die.' Tennyson, I think." Beverly shrugged her shoulders, obviously pleased by her cleverness and by Maggie's shocked look. "I called the police on you, too." Martin took one step forward, looking for all the world like he might punch Beverly and knock her wig to the wind.

Maggie reached for Martin's arm and smiled. She inhaled deeply and felt clarity ripple down her spine and straighten her thinking into a fine, sharp line. "Beverly Finker, you pathetic old bitch." Shaking her head, she puffed a little condescending laugh, the kind a prizefighter might give to his opponent on the ropes. "What are you, seventy? Seventy years old and still fighting the battle of the wallflower last picked at the high school dance. I remember you now. My mother talked about you. 'I wish that fat Finker woman would quit sending casseroles that aren't fit to feed to the dog. I'll be damned. If I eat these I'm sure to end up looking like a Finker fireplug, just like her daughter.'" Maggie licked her lips. "How could I have forgotten?"

Taking Martin's hand, she turned and over her shoulder said, "Fattie Finker, if you so much as pick up your phone and dial our number again I will slap your ass with a restraining order so confining you'll have to order your support hose online. And that, my dear, *will* be the talk of the town."

As Martin backed out of the Finker driveway, he looked admiringly at his wife. "Did your mother really say that?"

"Oh, hell no, honey. But sometimes you really have to take no prisoners."

## *It's Tough to Make Good Soup*

TWO YEARS LATER

Maggie pushed her jogging stroller up the front walk as she left a message for Eleanor on her cell phone. "The party starts around six thirty, and please don't bring a thing. It's Saturday; you get a break tonight."

Catching up with her, Julia jostled her own stroller up the walk with a wispy-headed boy sleeping in the seat, the collar of a red gingham shirt peeking over the top of a cotton blanket.

Maggie gently touched the boy's head. "Jack has the longest, prize-winning, supermodel eyelashes."

"Boys always do," Julia said, with a "life isn't fair" smirk on her face. "Perfect lean hips, beautifully defined calves, and never a ripple of cellulite in their tiny, shapely buttocks. Testosterone creates a swimsuit-ready body while they sleep." She traced a finger around her son's bread-dough elbow. "Men should be women. They could lie around looking beautiful and women could get the work done."

Maggie smiled in appreciation and Julia tucked the blanket snugly around her child's double chin. "I may only make boys, but they're pretty ones." Julia lifted her hair off the back of her neck and fanned her face. "Is Eleanor coming with your mom tonight? They've gotten close, haven't they?"

"She is and they have. They've a lot in common, if you know what I mean. Dead husbands, complicated kids, a love of gardening. She's bringing Edward, too," she said, widening her eyes with enjoyment.

Julia rocked her stroller and said, "I think it was the right decision not to confess everything that happened that summer. Some things truly are better left unsaid."

"I'm pretty sure Eleanor knows most of it, although she's never cornered me with it." While Maggie shoved the brake in place and unhooked Caitlyn from the safety restraints, she whispered a quick, "There you go." Her daughter waddled, hauling herself up the front steps, then turned back to look at Maggie before pointing with rosy indignation to the package wedged behind the screen door. Maggie called out, "Leave that, honey, I'll get it." The diaper bag swung free from her shoulder as she reached to pick up the padded envelope.

Maggie called out, "Martin."

"Here." Martin stepped into the living room wearing an apron that said *Cooking Jedi* on it.

Julia clicked her tongue with disdain. "Nice, Martin. Why not save time, and wear an apron that says *Dork* on it."

"Be nice, Julia. Martin can wear a batman suit if he's willing to cook."

"Does he have a batman suit?"

He kissed Maggie and bent to pick up Caitlyn, who was tottering unsteadily, having unhooked her jumpsuit and wound it around her ankles. "I spilled sauce on my super suit. I'm making spicy chicken wings."

"Hell, I'm just jealous. Last time Big Steven wanted to make an omelet he couldn't decide which egg to use."

Maggie turned to Martin. "Caitlyn's soaked. Could you change her and put her down for her nap? Julia and I are going to sit outside for a while."

"At your service, ladies," he said with not a drop of sarcasm. "Should I park this little guy in a quiet room, too?"

Julia nodded. "He's all yours, Jedi."

Outside, the women sat in two red Adirondack chairs in the shade of an old apple tree. The lighthearted sound of a songbird floated overhead.

"He's a doll, Maggie."

"Yeah, he is. It took him a little time to realize that 'I do' meant 'I will do . . . something other than nothing to keep this top twirling.' Plus, I had to open my eyes wide enough to notice that he needed a little direction. We both had work to do." Maggie untied and kicked off her running shoes. "Remember on our wedding day, when the priest read from First Corinthians? 'If I speak in the tongues of men and of angels, but have not love, I am only a resounding gong or a clanging cymbal.'" She rubbed her bare feet into the plush grass and tried to pick a dandelion with her toes. "If Martin has a flaw, it is his lack of clang and his ability to allow me free-range gonging."

"He's so sweet with Caitlyn. Big Steven doesn't get involved with the babies. He says it's because he's afraid he'll hurt them. I think it's because he gags at everything: poop, snot, food remnants. I've got just the opposite problem. If there's a mashed goldfish on Jack's sweater I'm wondering if I should offer it to the baby or eat it myself. Survival of the fittest."

"Ah, a mother's love." Maggie smiled. "Sometimes I like to fantasize about saving Caitlyn in strong, heroic ways. Like we're in midair above the Atlantic Ocean with a terrorist onboard, and I singlehandedly disarm and neutralize the threat with a drinking straw. I envision the headlines: 'A Mother's Love Saves Hundreds.'"

"Thinking like that will get you the presidency of the Neighborhood Watch."

"Yeah, I still need therapy, no doubt. But my therapist would have to be a quiet, placid woman with a frizzy salt-and-pepper bob and no awareness of hair gel."

Julia laughed and added, "She'd wear suede plum-colored Birkenstocks and have a signed photograph on the wall of Carole King singing 'Natural Woman.' Her office would smell of patchouli and there would be Kleenex boxes in macramé holders everywhere."

"I could cry and cry and all she'd ever say would be, 'You're right, of course, you're right.' Maybe she'd join in with some tears of her own."

"More likely, though, your HMO would assign you some self-righteous gay man who would be appalled by your conservative Junior League outfit."

Maggie nodded in agreement. "He'd crease his brow when I'd tell him about the vandalism. He'd make me write a letter to my long-dead father, forgive him, and then force me to confess to Eleanor. I'd probably have to pick up highway trash for a year."

Laughing and wiping her eyes with the corner of her T-shirt sleeve, Julia said, "What is a four-letter word for *no friggin' way*?"

Both women stopped talking and sat in the comfortable silence.

"During my labor, when I was so crazed with pain and fear, remember what I said to Martin?"

Julia nodded. "He told me. It's tough to make good soup."

"I was right. It is tough to make good soup." Maggie waved a fly away and somewhere in the distance a lawnmower started up. "I still get the urge to come clean to Eleanor sometimes. I take pride in my tidy hospital-cornered life and I climbed into a bed I couldn't make. There's stuff I still want to know."

"Like where he is and if he ever got married?"

With a doubtful expression on her face, Maggie said, "You're kidding. I didn't tell you this? He didn't get married. Eleanor says he moved to New York alone after visiting France and has been working on some big project."

"He didn't get married, huh. I guess I'm not that surprised." Julia squinted at Maggie. "What else do you know?"

"Nothing. I don't dare ask. I don't want to get into a conversation I can't get out of." She heaved a sigh. "Sometimes I replay my first conversation with him."

"But not in an obsessive way," Julia said.

Maggie shook her head and said, after a pause, "It's enjoyable. You know, I read once that a two-minute gaze at the opposite sex engenders feelings of romance and warmth." She remembered David's eyes on her again and swatted the feelings away, raising her hands to shoo a fly. "Do you suppose that it was just biology? Mammalian mating? I mean nothing says 'I don't like you' like moving out of town without a forwarding address."

"Mags, I think if you *had* kept in touch it would have indicated *less* feeling on his side. I'm willing to bet he didn't leave because of your little pranks. I think he knew he was in over his head."

"That seems farfetched. At this point, I guess we'll never know. And honestly, I don't care that much."

"I remember thinking in college that it would be great if it *was* all biology. There would be no unreturned phone calls, no hard feelings. All disinterested parties could blame their lack of attraction on pheromones. 'Your cake odor clashes with my summer sausage scent.' And there would still be plenty of time left on the answering machine for porn jokes."

"Never enough time for the porn jokes."

"What are you ladies deep in conversation about?" Martin walked toward them holding two tall glasses of lemonade.

"Men who smell like sausage."

Martin wrinkled his nose and sniffed under his armpit. "Fresh as a daisy. I brought you gals something to drink."

Julia stood. "You two take a breather from party preparations and sip here in the sun. I've got to take my boy and get out of here if we're all coming back for dinner." She looked at her watch. "Big Steven has reached his child-saturation point by now. I'm on borrowed time as it is."

"This is going to be a big block party if everyone who RSVP'd actually comes."

"You think anyone will miss the surveillance schedule, Mags?"

"Oh, shut up, Julia. Disbanding Neighborhood Watch was my idea, remember? Go home and make your famous brownies and try to get your butt here on time."

"I'll let myself out."

Martin eased himself into Julia's abandoned chair and sighed. "A potluck is definitely the way to go. All you need for a party then is a tablecloth and some paper plates. He took a large gulp of his lemonade and smiled. "Do you think Ella would have looked as much like you as Caitlyn does?"

"Hard telling. I like to think so. But Ella had your lips."

The phone rang inside and Martin started to stand. Maggie stopped him with a hand on his arm. "You sit. I'll get the phone and check on Caitlyn." The phone stopped ringing as she walked in the door and she veered toward her daughter's room. Stepping inside she could smell the mixture of fresh-baked bread and kid musk that was pure Caitlyn. Her daughter lay under her covers clutching her lovey dog, Bone-man, in a choke hold. She covered her child's head with her hand.

Closing the bedroom door, Maggie tiptoed back to the kitchen table. A sippy cup had tipped and there were two tiny drips of milk leaking from the seal. She picked up the package she had dislodged from the front door and examined it. Her name and address were written in a hand she did not recognize, and there was no return address anywhere. Maggie ripped the top of the package open and pulled a book free from the protective bubble wrap. She glanced inside for a note and found none, but a familiar face looked up at her from the back cover.

Unmistakably, David's unblinking eyes stared at her with the look she remembered from their first introduction at the kitchen sink. There it was: his smile, his hairline, his jaw, and the now-forgotten flurry of nerves at seeing him. She had first met him online, then in person, and now here he was in her hands, her thumb concealing his left earlobe.

She turned the book over and read its title: *On Maggie's Watch.* Puzzled, it took Maggie a minute to realize that David's photo was on the book because it was *his* book. He had written it. His name was right there on the cover: Craig David Tyson. She sat heavily in the kitchen chair and noticed a yellow tab marking a page. She opened the book, heard the familiar crack of the spine, and inhaled the new book smell. Then she read the inscription: *To Maggie: I understand more than you know and it's all right.* She swallowed hard.

She flipped to the book flap and read the copy. *Six months pregnant and the self-appointed president of her Neighborhood Watch program, Maggie discovers that her neighbors have secrets.*

Maggie's eyes drifted and her mind flashed to that day in the coffee shop, when she had almost divulged her own secrets and he had gently revealed his.

"He knew all along," she whispered to herself. "Holy crap." She remembered the tender way he had brushed her hair away from her face, his worried look on the ride home, the touch on her elbow. His words, "It's all right."

She scanned the remaining paragraphs on the book's shiny cover. *Maggie's veneer unravels as she begins to realize that her desire for control cannot make up for the knowledge that she may have been stalking the wrong man for the wrong reasons.*

Maggie ran her hand across David's photo. There was a flicker of longing in her chest, a lonely spark that was immediately extinguished as her husband moved into the kitchen. She tucked her head into his shoulder as he reached the back of the chair to hug her. He whispered, "Cuddlefish."

Then he glanced at the book. "What's this?" Martin asked.

"Nothing that can't wait," Maggie replied, tilting her chin back and kissing her husband's neck. "Caitlyn's sound asleep. What do you say we go upstairs and work on making another one just like her?"

# On Maggie's Watch

## READERS GUIDE

## *Discussion Questions*

1. The death of Maggie's first child has caused her to be overly cautious about her current pregnancy. Why do you think she insists on putting herself in harm's way and subjects herself to so much stress during her last trimester?

2. Julia and Maggie have very different ways of seeing the world. Maggie is fueled by a burning desire to seek out every possible danger while Julia rarely investigates below the surface of a situation. How do these points of view define the two women? Which point of view makes more sense and why?

3. Julia and Martin have a candid conversation about his ever-changing relationship with Maggie. He voices his expectations about marriage and family and explains how they differ from the realities of married life. How do these expectations and realities vary between the husbands and wives in the Finley and Morris households?

4. Ella's death has left an undeniable scar both on Maggie's and Martin's lives. How do they each deal with their grief? How do Maggie's coping methods console or confuse Martin?

5. Martin explains that he is working more hours so that he can take time off when his child is born. Maggie insists that he's growing distant and unsupportive during her time of need. How do you think men and women see pregnancy differently? Do you feel sympathetic to Martin's dilemma, or are Maggie's demands on him justified?

6. Julia becomes agitated when she discovers she is pregnant, while Maggie is ecstatic at the idea of starting a family. How do you think these women view children, and what are their reasons for having them?

7. The loss of a parent at an early age has shaped both Maggie and Julia in their adult lives. Are they more similar or different because of it? How does this traumatic experience affect their interactions with their own family and loved ones?

8. Communication differences between the sexes are a constant theme throughout the novel. How does each

male character communicate differently with his partner or his friends in this story? Does one man stand out as a better communicator than the others? Why?

9. What fuels Maggie's attraction to David? Would the sexual tension between them exist if she weren't pregnant? Do you think Maggie ever entertained the idea of betraying her husband prior to her discovery of David's true identity?

10. Maggie visits the Tyson home multiple times, committing acts of vandalism that escalate in magnitude over the course of the novel. Despite the fact that Eleanor declines to press charges against her, do you feel that Maggie should be punished for her actions? Why or why not?

11. Steven feels that Maggie is a stressful influence on Julia. We learn that while Maggie hasn't always been there for Julia, Julia remains Maggie's most loyal confidant. Why do you think Julia remains dedicated to Maggie when their relationship is so obviously unbalanced? Do you feel that Maggie takes Julia for granted? If so, why? Which other characters are undervalued or made to feel unappreciated by a friend, lover, or relative?

12. How does The American Dream or, in Maggie's own words, "The American Median," impact her outlook on her marriage, her pregnancy, and her neighborhood?

13. Are online resources like the Department of Corrections website's list of sexual predators a blessing or a curse to neighborhoods like Elmwood, Wisconsin?

14. Whether it's her mother, her best friend, or her husband, Maggie seems to be surrounded by voices of reason. How would their absence affect the outcome of this novel? Who do you feel has the most influence on Maggie's behavior? Does this change throughout the story?